BISTRA JOHNSON

TALES FROM
THE FUTURE

ISBN: 978-0-9556875-1-8

If you go along the picturesque Cote d'Azur in search of "Elounda", the Provençal house, depicted in the following narrative, you are not going to find it. Yet it exists; in another dimension, or in a parallel Universe, there is a villa "Elounda", exactly as described. The people that reside in it similarly exist in a different timeline. It's unlikely that you will ever meet them, but who knows, they might, just might pay you an unexpected visit one day to return yours.

This is not exactly the saga of the "Elounda" family. Accept it rather as glimpses into the lives of some of those connected with the place at different points of its existence. Those are people who left a most distinctive mark on it and a lasting legacy and maybe were in turn influenced to a certain extent by "Elounda".

Welcome to "Elounda"s World!

CONTENTS

A Russian doll. With a little enigmatic smile frozen on her wooden face. Hardly a Mona Lisa, and yet so mysterious. Will you dare to open her and discover her secrets? If you do, you will find that there is another, a smaller one nestled inside her and another one and another one. Inside her there are hidden an infinite number of nested Russian dolls. But then when you place them back inside each other, there remains just the original one – this brightly coloured Matrioshka with her cryptic and somewhat ironic smile. What is this disdainful lady trying to tell you? And if she did, would you understand her? And yet – you want to know the secret. You are going to seek it out come what may. There is a whole world hidden there waiting for you in all its four spatial dimensions and perhaps she holds the key to it. Or at least that's what you are led to believe.

A mere human and therefore - as a three dimensional being, your perceptions are somewhat limited. One lifetime is hardly enough even just to get a glimpse. How then are you going to fully appreciate this vast and complex Universe? How are you going to cope with such an abstract notion as the space-time continuum, which even if undetected, never the less exists?

There are a myriad worlds to discover out there and you are just at the start of your journey. Where is it going to take you? You will open the next page thinking that it's the beginning, but is it really? Here and now is the Present. There is always something back in the Past and always something waiting in the Future.

PRELUDE

Cross-legged in the classical "Lotus" pose on the transparent floor of her all transparent spherical home, Titania was meditating. She was gazing at the green expanse outside, her eyes unblinking, but she wasn't seeing any of it, her mind was busy on some rather indefinable issues; her place in the Universe for a start.

Since examining her family tree records for the first time earlier that day, a subtle change was taking place in the mind of this frustrated and temperamental but otherwise brilliant young woman. Up till now, boredom and depression had hampered her achievement rates considerably. For the first time in her life she felt centred, focused; she experienced a sense of belonging that she had never known before.

Wasn't it wonderful? Wasn't she lucky? What a chance to originate from such a renowned family! And this explained certain things about her personality too; now it all fitted together nicely. Had she known that earlier...But there was no point to dwell on her past failures. The future was ahead of her, a Future with a capital F! The motto of that particular day, which had flashed across the screen at the time of her early morning wake-up call, was fitting: "Don't cry over spilt milk!"(whatever "milk" was supposed to be, something extinct, long gone by the looks of it), but the general meaning seemed to indicate that she shouldn't regret for anything. Besides it was not too late yet...

A slight smile appeared on Titania's pale lips, those same lips reputed not to have known what a smile was. The pain she had felt the day before yesterday seemed far away now. Someone she had trusted, someone she had valued, had betrayed her. Telling an untruth, for her, equalled a betrayal.

How small and insignificant it all seemed today. In view of the great revelations, she had just had, her past itself looked somewhat faded: the injustices she had fought against, the offences she had suffered from, the hopelessness she had often felt – what was all that for? The fact was that someone as supersensitive as she was, should have learned a lot earlier how to cope better with these little annoyances, that life was so full of.

Titania had started recently to do yoga in an attempt to relieve her stress, something, she was pleased to say, that was definitely working for her. She rose slowly from her "lotus" position. The transparency of the material her home was built of, made it look as if she was levitating in mid air, but this was of course, pure illusion. Naturally nobody was there to witness her acrobatics because in those times people were not supposed to wander about on foot in areas not designated for the purpose of leisure or sport and trespassing was unheard of. So Titania was left in peace while doing her routine yoga exercises with a mind still following her previous train of thought.

What next, was the obvious question of course. She had to complete her education first of all; the education, she had so badly neglected. But then what? She had all these ideas, floating chaotically round her head, about what she wanted to do next. Suddenly out of this entire and seemingly endless range of possibilities, so overwhelming to her before, there slowly started to emerge and to take shape, a clear notion about what her vocation was going to be. It was as simple as that! How hadn't she thought about it earlier? But then earlier she was too busy being angry with the rest of the Universe, too busy and thus denying herself the happiness and fulfilment just within her reach!

Once, long time ago she had written an essay on what questions she would have asked a certain famous historical personality if she had the chance to interview them. With the overconfidence of youth she had written in the end: "I'll go back in time and just do it!" Now she wanted to do that more than ever. The personality in question in fact turned out to be related to her. She had seen him so many times via the Link, she had even visited his home on the coast, now a museum, but it just wasn't the same. Titania had always wanted to meet him in person.

"Was it a coincidence," she wondered, "to have chosen him as the subject of my essay? Is it possible that a blood bond could reveal itself like that? At least it would explain my profound interest in him and more importantly in his work. Certain aptitudes must be inherited. Didn't they argue at one stage about nature or nurture? Well, nowadays they say its nurture that matters the most and yet why do they care so much about the genetic material? I think it's not just a question of the physical health of the individual, although that's obviously extremely important. What they won't admit is that there is a careful selection where the embryos are concerned. Funny I never thought of this before."

Nightfall and the transparent walls of Titania's home had now become opaque, at least from the outside. From the interior she was still able to look out in the darkness and see the moon and the stars.

Titania stood still for a moment, gazing at Orion, the Hunter, the one they say, who challenged the gods.

"Have they been trying to create a super-race? And why do I say "they" anyway, when it is us! Alright, not me personally, not even my generation, but our elders, who are in any case part of humankind. I hope they haven't bitten off more than they can chew."

Shaking her head, still deep in thought, Titania continued with her yoga exercises.

PROLOGUE OR EPILOGUE
It's up to the reader to decide which

The day has come when I am finally prepared to act. I am no longer willing just to sit back and watch events unfolding in front of my eyes without taking part in any of them myself whatsoever. What's going to happen when I interfere? I have no idea. But now I have the means to do it and by Jove, I will! I don't really care if this turns my whole life upside down.

What is there to lose really? Even my life has become worthless to me now. The question is: should I believe all I hear from the Future? Perhaps not, but at the moment I desperately need to hang on to something. In the end humankind hasn't changed a lot throughout its long history. We've always expected some guidance from above and we still do. "Nothing new under the sun" is still as valid a maxim as it always has been.

All right! At the risk of sounding superstitious, I'll listen to the voices from the Future. In times past, my ancestors indulged in spiritual séances and trusted what the spirits of the dearly departed had to say to them. What I am doing is not that different at all. I'll listen to what my unborn descendants have to say and if, only if, I consider it sensible, I might try to set up that Link with the past. And the Chain will be established once and for ever. It would be a sort of logical conclusion to what one of my ancestors once started. A Chain reaction?!

I experienced the Link for the first time when I was 16; like everybody. Now it all seems a long, long time ago. We were all gathered, I remember in the Chrono-Bridge Centre; that is all who had the same birth date. We were excited but understandably apprehensive too. We were giggling

9

nervously, exchanging silly jokes or just posturing about in a typical adolescent fashion. Oh, the naiveté of youth! Yet I cherish those memories more than anything else in my life. But I digress.

Back there in the Chrono-Bridge Centre we were installed in cubicles and given step by step instructions how to proceed. I put on my COM link helmet and entered the time I had selected according to the instructions. Then it all commenced. I was pulled in a vortex of some sort where up and down, left and right, had lost their meaning, it was like being hurled out in space, spiralling out of control, only it wasn't actually space as such, it was time.

The giddiness that followed was almost unbearable, but it stopped almost as soon as it started and all of a sudden I found myself in a slider craft wharf of the past. If this was indeed the date and the time I had entered, I would be able to encounter one of my illustrious ancestors at a time prior to the moment when Fame smiled on him. Having the sensation of a disembodied spirit, I just hovered about looking curiously at the old fashioned technology, lying around. I've studied history of course, and yet I was somewhat taken aback by those primitive vehicles. Was it really true that those were the prototypes of the sophisticated beauties we have today?

My musings were interrupted by the arrival of yet another slider craft which looked much more aerodynamic and more pleasing to the eye than the others. I thought it was coming to get me, forgetting that the pilot cannot possibly be aware of my presence and more to the point, I was not actually there, not in body in any case.

Presently the craft was brought to a standstill and out of it emerged two people – a tall handsome male with greying temples in whom I recognised my great- great- etc. grandfather and an attractive female who must have been about his age (if she was who I thought she must be), but looked definitely younger: Julian and Sophie. At long last I had met them.

The next moment without any warning I found myself dwelling in Julian's body, not that it bothered him at all, for he never knew, but for me it was rather disconcerting. There I was, a 16 year old boy in the body of this mature man that I had always admired, holding the hand of my beautiful great-great- etc. grandmother! It was difficult to adjust myself to this situation, but I did as well as I could and was even able to follow their brief exchange.

"Don't come with me to the terminal, Julian," said Sophia, "it's pointless and a waste of time. I'm just going away for the day and I really dislike prolonged goodbyes."

"Are you sure you don't want me to come? Not even to accompany you to the terminal?" Julian insisted, "I understand that you don't like me to turn up at the Adapt centre, but…"

"Please, Julian, don't! I've made up my mind. Don't worry, I am used to coping with difficult circumstances. I appreciate your support, but it's all right. I would rather go on my own and face it. If all goes well, Sylvia will be coming to stay with us very soon. You'll have all the time in the world to get acquainted and to get used to each other."

"My dear, you know pretty well it's not this that bothers me…"

"I know. Kiss me, Julian! Now I have to go. You'll be here to collect me on my return?"

"Of course. Good luck!"

She got into the transporter and was gone. Julian lingered, looking rather anxious and I stayed with him of course, thinking: "So that's how it had happened. They must've been quite uneasy about it all at the time. But then facing the unknown is always like that. I knew the upshot of it so for me it was a bit like watching a film after seeing the ending beforehand; the characters there agonising about some issue or another, the outcome of which I already knew."

Later I was back at the Relate Centre still incredulous but pleased with what I had witnessed. That was my first experience of the Link. It gave me a new sense of identity, it made me realise for the first time that I was a link myself in a long chain of human development. The whole experience was a sort of initiation ritual and remained forever ingrained in my mind.

I was determined to pursue a career in the same field as Julian and explore all the possibilities, he'd opened for us. I firmly believed that if I put my mind to it I would succeed. The disillusionment that came later was inevitable.

We've become a rather decadent society, overindulging ourselves rather than striving to further improve our lot. We've entered a period of stagnation. The Time-Bubble Theory has lost its appeal and stepped out of the limelight to open the way for new inventions aimed exclusively at entertainment. As the necessary funds for research in my field were limited, I had to content myself with getting involved in projects that did not inspire me at all and got myself into a real rut. Years passed.

Finally one day I decided enough was enough. I had saved some money, so I retired with my wife and son to my old Provencal house, home to our family for generations, and started the research I always wanted to do. It wasn't easy, I had my setbacks and at least a couple of times seriously considered abandoning the project. But eventually my persistence paid off. I had a breakthrough! I managed to come up with a means of sending communications to the Past! At first this success filled me with pure joy. I just couldn't believe my luck. Then sobering thoughts started to fill my mind. Was that going to be wise? What was I trying to accomplish? What if it proved disastrous? To meddle with the Past is not a trifling matter.

Disaster struck anyway before I even had the chance to set up my experiment. Fate itself, it seemed, had taken a hand in the matter. My wife and son lost their lives together with hundreds of others when the sea attacked the shore with hurricane force in the resort below; a day in the amusement arcade ended up in tragedy.

Naturally I was devastated. I still can't bear to look at their portraits or to meet them through the Link. I started to follow Julian and family instead. They also have now gone to this other dimension that we call Afterlife, but from my point of view they have always belonged there. My encounters with them have always been through the Link. However seeing my wife and son through the same medium was extremely painful. To experience again and again moments of our life together – happy and sad was almost unbearable. I badly wanted them back in my real life, but they were gone forever. So I got myself totally involved in the life of Julian's family instead of dealing with my own bereavement.

When yesterday I was approached from the Future and encouraged to carry on with my experiment, which I had abandoned, I welcomed the opportunity. What the hell! I've always wanted to do that so I'd better just get on with it and not bother about the consequences. Even if things go wrong, I would not know the difference, I won't know it in any case, for once I've changed the past, I would've automatically changed my own life already. I better go now and face the music!

THE RIVER OF TIME

She stood on the cliff, binoculars in her hand, looking at the sea. In the late afternoon, under the last rays of the sun, her hair was a crown of fire. She stood there, motionless, unaware of the tall, big man, who was watching her. In the end, he glanced at his watch and moved towards her.

"Hello," his voice startled her and she almost dropped her binoculars, "I didn't mean to scare you, I'm sorry. My name is Julian, Julian Bradley. I am here for the regatta."

He had a pleasant, well-modulated voice and a nice smile, which reassured her and she smiled back.

"Sophia Leonard. Usually I'm not so jumpy, but then I didn't expect anybody here, at this time of day..."

"You are probably wondering whether I am lost. Not exactly. I thought I might get a better view from up here, which seems to be the case. And I wanted another glimpse of the house there, the one called "Elounda". The locals tell me it is the oldest house in the area."

She looked in the direction where he was pointing, but did not answer immediately. When she spoke, there was hesitation in her voice.

"Just an old mansion. Who cares anyway. You are not a ghost hunter or something, are you?"

"No, no. Do I look like one? No, just interest in architecture. 20th century architecture especially."

He knew that this would attract her attention and was not mistaken. But the result was not what he'd expected or what he hoped for.

"Nice to meet you, Julian. But it is getting late. And I have to go."

"Would you allow me to walk you home? You see, I am here on my own for the weekend..."

"Look, I don't know what you expected when you approached me, but whatever it was, it is not going to work. Good bye."

"I've messed it all up, it's not going to work," thought Julian almost in panic.

She turned to go and he realised, that there was no time to waste, he was running short of it; he abandoned the carefully prepared plan and grabbed her hand.

"Please, stay. I have to speak to you. It is important."

She waited in silence for him to continue.

"All right. I wasn't exactly honest with you. I know all about you. I know that you value your privacy so much that you wouldn't let anybody close to you ever since... sorry again, I shouldn't talk about that. It is none of my business and this is not what I want to talk to you about, anyway. It is just...I don't know where to start from."

Under those piercing blue eyes, he felt very unsure of himself. What did he expect from her? A mere stranger, to barge in on her like that. Especially when he knew her story, the recent loss of her husband, killed in that dreadful accident, while piloting the passenger ship on its way to Mars. That was the top news for more than a week. And then later, after the investigations when it came clear, that not enough safety precautions had been taken for cost saving reasons, not enough investment made, where human lives were at stake. And the firm involved got away with blue murder. They paid a hefty fine, true, but the hundreds who died, could not be brought back to life again. She had the right to be angry. He wondered what more he could say. Apparently, she'd made up her mind:

"Oh well, whatever it is, it could wait till tomorrow. Give me a ring. 11 o'clock."

And she was gone. That was so unexpected that he remained there a long time still asking himself was that a success, or a failure. But she had promised to listen to his story, and that was a beginning.

Julian was making his way through a crowd of people, trying to reach the room where his equipment was supposed to be. Those people seemed to be constantly in the way, some of them wearing strange old fashioned costumes. He wondered vaguely if this wasn't a fancy dress party though he didn't remember it being described as such in the invitation. The invitation! He couldn't recollect if he had received an invitation to be there at all. Slightly worried, he continued his way. His worry increased when he realised that he was walking past wax figures instead of humans, or perhaps they were just people in suspended animation? Maybe the whole place was an enchanted castle, waiting for him to come and end the spell. He entered a door opened especially for him to see all his equipment arranged in the room and the slight figure of a stranger standing there perfectly immobile. Julian was lost for words, but just then the stranger turned towards him and a pair of beautiful blue eyes framed by long, mahogany-red hair, calmly looked him in the face.

Julian woke up with a start. He must've been dreaming! What a weird dream that was and so vivid! He got up quickly, realising that it was getting late and he had to get ready for the promised interview with Sophia Leonard.

An hour later Julian was standing in front of the house, with hands in his pockets. He had just been admitted through the gates, which to his relief meant that he was expected. The house, a typical Provençal holiday home, decorated in warm washed colour tones, the way they've always done it in the South, appeared peaceful and quiet under the midmorning sun. It seemed a lot bigger than he anticipated and not exactly welcoming: front door, shutters, patio doors were all closed as if the inhabitants had already left before the end of the season. There was a name plate above the front door which read "Villa Elounda". Unsure, Julian made a step towards that door and it suddenly opened for him as the whole house, shutters and all, suddenly became alive, awoken from its slumber. Sophia came forward to meet him; touching his hand in a friendly gesture, she motioned him in.

They sat on a big sunny covered terrace in the grounds of the house, with the sound of the sea as background music. Sophia was wearing a silver-coloured dress and her eyes looked more grey than blue.

"I checked up on you," she said, very business-like. "You are a physicist and I don't know where this interest in architecture or in my house comes into it?"

"Yes, I am a physicist and I have indeed an interest in architecture. My father was an architect. And a good one too. He built the new Broadstairs complex in the La Manche District."

"John Bradley was your father?" she seemed impressed. "That is interesting. But you have to tell me your story."

"As you found out, I am a physicist, I am doing research in connection with the Fourth Dimension Theory and my colleague and I stumbled upon some space/time-continuum anomalies."

"Wait now!" interrupted Sophia. "You've realised that I am not a physicist and I know very little on the matter. Why not take it easy and slow, so I could grasp the picture. You are talking about travelling in time? You've got a crazy machine, we get in it, go back to the past, change history and so on."

Julian smiled:

"No, I don't think this could ever work. And besides it would involve a hell of a lot of energy to transport a human being in time, not withstanding the whole lot of other problems that could arise from there. No, I am talking about glimpses into the past and probably even into the future, using the space/time-continuum "bubble" concept, on which I am currently working. This particular phenomenon could be used to give us a different perspective of the past. These so called "time bubbles" appear at particular points and at particular times; there seems to be a pattern. I've calculated all this; you could look at my calculations if you are good at maths, oh well, never mind that. In any case, at a certain location, which happens to be situated in your house, I predict such an occurrence next week. I want to take advantage of it. My aim is the projection of pure consciousness in time. I've got the necessary equipment. All I need is your cooperation in this matter. It is a very important experiment and probably my whole career depends on it. Will you help me?"

The so called Video Room was huge, elliptical and very stylishly furnished. They had just gone through some old records and films about "Elounda", the way the house was in the old days and were discussing how well preserved it was. Julian had moved to the mansion the day before and had already set up his apparatus while waiting for the right time. They were able to indulge themselves in discussing other topics and in finding similar interests.

Architecture was just one of them. They had a little dispute about the style, in which "Elounda" had been built. Julian insisted it was influenced by the Frank Lloyd Wright style and Sophia reckoned that it was built in the traditional Provençal style, some features of which it undoubtedly had. Sophia underlined the un-European character of Wright's architecture, but Julian argued that his concept was human harmony with nature, giving the example of the famous Waterfall House.

In the end they spent hours looking at the old records and plans and found out a lot of interesting information, which even Sophia was unaware of. She knew though that "Elounda" was built by one of her ancestors, who had been an architect himself, and her family had resided there ever since. They were so engrossed in this occupation, that they did not notice how late it was.

"I should really go and do some more work," said Julian, "check a few parameters, ensure that it is going to work, the way it is supposed to. It is a nerve-wracking business, you know."

"You promised to tell me some more about it!"

"Yes, but I've just been wondering isn't it a better idea, if you experienced it, without being briefed beforehand, an unprejudiced witness, so to speak."

"To experience it! Are you telling me that you will allow me to take part in it?" Sophia clasped her hands in excitement and Julian thought how different she was now from the melancholic woman that he'd met only a few days ago.

"Of course, I couldn't do it without you. I will rely very much on your assistance."

"Oh, that's great! I wonder what we are going to see. Is it going to be like a film of something that has happened ages ago? You said we could not change the past, could we?"

"Not exactly like a film, no. It would be rather like seeing through the eyes of somebody else, somebody, who lived in a different time. Don't worry, they won't even be aware of our presence and we would not be able to influence this person, or change a thing even if we wanted to. And we shouldn't try, either. It might be dangerous. Remember, you asked me if I was a ghost hunter. In a way this is what we are going to be - hunting the shadows of the past. And if you ask me, I think, that this is what ghosts really are - nothing to be scared of. They most likely appear in such places, such "bubbles", where time could go both ways; somebody just stumbles into a "time-bubble" and sees people wearing outlandish clothes, behaving in a strange way and there you are, this is how ghost stories appear."

"Fascinating!"

"It is, isn't it? I was interested in this, since I was a child. Read lots of stories on this topic. I had this idea of time being like a river, you never could be in the same river twice, as they say, could you? And then this river has a current, which takes you to the sea, or wherever. It is difficult, if not impossible to swim against the current, but again, there might be some short cuts and other tricks, because it doesn't flow in a straight line, it meanders."

"What do you mean by "meanders"?" asked Sophia mystified.

"Well, don't you remember Einstein's theory? Think of the four dimensions. The time-space continuum is not actually linear although we perceive it as such, but curved and this curvature is a result of influence of mass against movement in time..." Julian checked himself seeing her blank expression and added: "I know, I know, it is far too difficult to grasp, sorry! But believe me, there are short cuts, because of the way space is bent and we are going to find one!"

"Fine! I trust you. You have already convinced me. It sounds rather crazy, but what the hell! Let's go for it and see...see for example how this house was built! We had this dispute, didn't we? Let's see who's right! Can we do that?"

"Hmm, I think we might be able to, if you know the dates...Look, let me go and do some thinking and a few more calculations. Can I use the study?"

"Of course, Julian. Dinner is at 7:00. See you then."

Julian was busy with his gadgets, checking some dials, readjusting some connections. Sophia didn't have a clue what he was doing, and felt that she was in his way. But he had said that he wanted her there and she waited patiently. She was sitting in a comfortable chair in the conservatory and was trying to read, but her mind kept wandering.

She thought that in fact there was no conservatory, when "Elounda" was first built. She had found out, that part of it was a dining area with a view towards the sea, part of it - an open terrace - patio as they used to call it. It seems that the climate was a lot hotter then; especially in these parts and an open terrace was what everybody had at the time. Sophia was able to find out quite a lot about that epoch.

Being a historian gave her access to a lot of info-sources and in any case, she was used to doing research accessing the Archives and she didn't waste a minute. Of course, there were quite a lot of "white" areas, lost documentation etc, so she felt like trying to put together a puzzle, but some of the bits were missing.

Anyway, a later renovation of the house had been done. Walls had been knocked down; the terrace had been enclosed and became a conservatory, though it was still used for a dining room every now and then for more informal occasions. Sophia and Julian had already had their dinner here, but now the area was cleared of most of the furniture and Julian was preparing his experiment.

There wasn't a lot of time left and Sophia was glancing frequently at her watch. At last it was all set and they sat opposite each other and tried to make themselves comfortable. They had to put bizarre looking sets of headphones on their heads, with little aerials, sticking in the air, which Sophia found hilarious.

"That is enough," said Julian, trying unsuccessfully to hide his smile, "let's concentrate now, because the "show" is about to begin. You have this little button there, to press, if you want to be disconnected. You can hear my voice in your headphones, I can hear yours. Don't worry; you are not going to interfere with anybody's thoughts, you will just see through their eyes. They would never know that you were even there. Wow, it's beginning!"

They felt, like being pulled into a whirlpool, almost to the point of losing consciousness, then dizziness, and then after a period, which seemed as long as eternity, they found themselves on a sunny hill, starring at the sea.

Nothing had changed, they thought, but then they realised slowly that it had. The view towards the sea, looked the same, but in fact it wasn't. The town below had shrunk to a tiny village to the benefit of the beach, which stretched for quite a distance. Sophia thought afterwards that she should compare it later with the old films and photos that she had.

"I don't quite feel my body," she said. "I wonder is this normal, probably this is how a free spirit would feel, or maybe I am dead, electrocuted or something by your bloody machine, Julian, are you there, Julian?"

"Don't shout, for Heaven's sake. Of course, I am not there, that's why you couldn't see me. I am here with you. Calm down. You cannot feel your body, I cannot feel mine either. There's nothing to worry about. You cannot go hundreds of years back in time and feel like you are going for a walk in your back garden!"

"Hundreds of years! Oh dear! Julian! So we've made it! We've made it!"

Then they saw the vehicle. It was an odd looking one and Sophia remembered that she had actually seen such on some very, very old film footage. But this was a real one and it was approaching them fast.

"What on earth is that?" exclaimed Julian.

"It is an old car. This is how they used to call them."

"It seems pretty new to me. But ugly, very ugly and primitive."

"Yeap. They didn't have the technology in those days, Julian."

"It's pathetic to transport yourself from place to place like that, isn't it?"

"I suppose it is. But they didn't think that way. In earlier centuries they were even using horse-drawn carriages".

"Now you've said it, I remember it. From my history lessons. But it sounds unbelievable."

"Oh, it's going to run me over! Juliaaan!"

"You panic too much, Sophie. Stay still. You haven't got a body there to be run over, remember? What is happening though?"

"Julian! It is exactly as you said. I can see now through her eyes. What a weird feeling. Are you sure she can't hear me?"

"Ah, I see! I obviously use this man's senses, and you..."

"It is him! The architect! I looked up in the archives, remember! Oh my God, we are there, we are really, truly there! He was one of my ancestors. The one who built the house. The house! It's disappeared, of course, the house that he *is* going to build."

"You wanted to see this, didn't you? But listen! What are they talking about? I can't understand a thing."

"Your ear is not attuned to their speech, but you probably will get some sense of it, if you listen carefully, Julian. It is one of the old languages. It's English. They used to speak it exactly in the lands where you come from. They didn't have the Universal language then, that came later. In any case, Universal is based on English and a few others, like French, and Spanish and German."

"It's beautiful here," the woman, whom the man was calling Zara was saying, "and so peaceful, too."

"It's just the spot. It's ours and I am going to build here a little castle for you!"

"Yes, I know what you English say - my home is my castle! I just want a house, a nice little house, overlooking the sea; maybe a swimming pool."

"Of course we ought to have a swimming pool. But we'll build the house first. We've taken the first step, we bought the land. It's a start. Look, I've brought a bottle of champagne! Let's celebrate!"

They took out of the car a tartan blanket and a picnic basket and sat down on the ground. Julian and Sophia had seen such things in films, but never actually had a real picnic themselves. The climate was not so mild in their time and people in general didn't like to have their meals outdoors. So for them it was a revelation, for they were actually taking part in all this.

The couple shared their bottle of champagne and obviously enjoyed it.

"I couldn't taste it at all! It's not fair, I love champagne," remarked Sophia disappointedly. "We should open one later."

They also had some unfamiliar foods, which neither Sophia, nor Julian recognised. Then the man opened a little white box with some writing on it and offered it to the woman. She took a small cylindrical object out of it (it seemed to be made out of dried herbs, wrapped with white paper) and placed it in her mouth.

"I really shouldn't do this," she said, "neither should you, Philip!"

The man took a tiny metal gadget out of his pocket and pressed it. A flame appeared on the surface and he offered it to the woman, who approached her head, still with the little cylindrical object in her mouth, which encountering the flame, started to smoulder. She inhaled deeply and with obvious pleasure and then the man said:

"It is all this health campaign business! Bad for your health, rubbish! The only reason, I am going to stop smoking, is because they are becoming so bloody expensive, that's why. All the tax they put on it!"

"What are they doing?" asked Julian, who was trying in vain to understand their exchange and their actions.

"They are smoking cigarettes. You know, tobacco..."

"Oh, so this is how it was, how interesting! I knew about tobacco smoking of course, but somehow didn't imagine it exactly like that. They look quite healthy though..."

"Julian, it wasn't that dangerous, not the tobacco; it was the drugs, that were the problem at the time. The remedy that cured that problem was discovered a lot later and before that lots of people were dependant on them. But let me listen, I didn't quite catch it. She is going to Sofia and he could join her this time, he doesn't need a visa any more. What visa? Is she talking about credit? No, that doesn't sound right. No, no, no, in fact it's about visa requirements! Going from one place to another, they still had this in the 20th century and well into the 21st. It must've been horrible to seek permission every time you wanted to cross borders!"

"But I thought that they had a democratic society then! The rights of men! Free movement and all that!" Julian expostulated.

"So they said, but in practice citizens from poorer parts of the world were not free to travel wherever they wanted. The Eastern sector for example. But yes! She came from there, didn't she? It all comes back to me now: Zara was born in Sofia and she needed visas to be able to travel and live abroad."

Sophia was trying to remember what else she had found in the family records without missing anything from the interesting dialogue taking place:

"Listen! They are discussing a visit to Sofia later that year. But first they have to get back to Kent, where was that, oh yes – Britain, The La Manche Peninsula! And what? They are going to drive all the way in this stupid vehicle and go to a tunnel to cross the Channel?! Let me think! When was The Great Dyke built? A lot later, I should think. The Dutch built it to link the British Islands to the Old Continent. But before that, there was indeed a Channel tunnel, otherwise they had to ferry those vehicles across La Manche. And they were using fuel, petrol. Do you hear that? Petrol prices are rising, says Philip. There is a strike. The French want lower fuel prices. They might have problems on the way."

Sophia's voice sounded excited while she pursued her line of thought:

"How interesting! You see evidence of all this in the old records, but you just accept it as a fact, and it is not as simple as that! Those inefficient, stupid vehicles are using petrol, polluting the environment and all they are thinking of, is fuel prices!"

25

"But of course, that was their means of transport! What else do you expect?" Julian remarked. "It must've been even before the time they started to use pressurised air as a substitute for fuel. 21st century, I think it was. So it's imminent. The high fuel prices are going to encourage them to look for substitutes. Fascinating! But they are changing the subject now. There, we can see some sketches of the house at long last."

"That's the plan of the first floor," Philip was saying. "Look, here is the kitchen and here - the dining room, facing south, towards the sea, it's what you wanted, isn't it? To be able to have your meals while enjoying the panorama out of the French windows, or to sit outside, weather permitting. The sitting room will also have a sea view. But the library has to be in the back, I am afraid."

"Yes, I suppose. You can't have all the rooms facing south. Besides the library is a place where you have to concentrate on your reading, not admiring the views," agreed Zara.

Philip resumed his explanations:

"And then I will make good use of this slope; you will be able to get directly to the second floor from the side entrance here. We'll have to form terraces because it's rather steep, but it's not a problem. We'll even put a swimming pool."

"That will be nice, but I think we should concentrate on the house first. Once we finish it, we'll think about swimming pools and gardens etc."

"That goes without saying, darling. I just wanted you to see the whole picture. The way it's going to be in the future. Because it will take time you know. Rome wasn't built in a day, as they say. And I have my day job too. But look at my plan now. You like it? Here is the entrance and the staircase leading to the second floor, where the bedrooms will be. And a sky -light above the staircase. Solar panels on the roof. See? Environmentally friendly as you always wanted. Can you visualise it?"

"Oh yes!" Sophia exclaimed, forgetting where she was, then, embarrassed, bit her lip.

Zara looked at Philip's solemn face and decided to tease him a little:

"No, unless you use some computer graphics to make it clear," then added, seeing a shade of impatience in his expression. "I'm just pulling your leg, Philip! Of course I can see it. Isn't it exactly what we always dreamed of? And the stairs will be wooden, yes? The floor – terracotta; probably marble would be better, oh, I don't know...in any case, it's not going to be less stylish, than the one you showed me in your magazine, the Waterfall House! If anything, I think it looks better, at least on paper!"

"Wait and see! But I am sure, you will love it!"

"And we'll name it "Elounda"…what do you say, darling? Do you remember our time in Elounda?"

"How can I ever forget?" replied Philip gently. "Elounda"? Why not? It's as good a name as any."

The sun was going down. Zara's hair looked almost red and Julian remembered the day when he met Sophia on the hillside. He didn't think before that there was any particular resemblance between the two women, but he wasn't so sure now...

And then it was all over. They sat quietly for a while till they got back to their senses.

"I need a drink," said Julian eventually. "You're all right?"

"I'm fine. Julian! Did this really happen? Or was it just a dream?" she paused. "Let's find the champagne!"

And later when the bottle was almost finished:

"It wasn't as old as theirs, but it was the best I ever had!"

"If it was so old it couldn't possibly taste so good!" remarked Julian.

"I don't know about you, but the next trip I'm going for, is going to be there, to this Sofia Metropolis! Funny, I've never been there before, but now, when I know, I am reminded that my roots are there..."

Julian looked at her, lifting his eyebrows:

"The Balkans - who knows, there might appear another "time-bubble" at some point; anything is possible, and if so, I could join you there and we could have another time-adventure, even more exciting than this one!"

And Sophia thought: "Why not, anything is possible."

The question was, had all this really happened or was it some elaborate plot, a cure, her therapist came up with, to help her overcome her depression? Whatever it was, it worked and she didn't want to question it. Despite everything it was so sweet to be still alive, to see, to feel, this big wonderful world around!"

FACE TO FACE WITH YOUR ANCESTOR

Sophia had a videophone call, which she took in her study. She didn't come back for some time and Julian wondered what had happened, some bad news perhaps. He was sitting in the conservatory and listening to some soothing music, which he found in the music terminal. It was the end of a hard week for him and he desperately needed some rest. He was almost asleep, when Sophia finally came back, but made an effort to rouse himself.

"So, what is the news then?"

He noticed that she was very pale.

"I have some news, alright, probably the biggest news, that one can imagine. Only I am not sure whether to be upset or happy. I am just in a state of shock."

"Your rich aunt died and left you a fortune?" asked Julian, pouring her a glass of water.

"It is actually the other way round. My long lost great-great-great aunt came back to life and what she is going to bring me, is not clear yet. One thing I know for sure, we are going to see a lot of each other. It seems that I am her closest living relative."

"You are joking, right?" asked Julian, incredulous.

"I wish I was. But this is what they've just told me. She is very much alive, will have to spend a few days in the Adapt Centre and I could either go and meet her there, or she will be brought here to stay with me."

"And how old is she?"

"Or how young, depends how you look at these things. She is only fifteen."

Julian was about to ask again if she was joking, but then he thought better of it and bit his lip.

"Have you met her before?" he asked instead.

"I know of her from all the research I've done on my family tree. But that's all. Look Julian, it is an unbelievable story. I wish I was a writer, what a golden opportunity I am missing! But let's stick to the facts, I'm a historian and this is what I do best. You remember Zara, from our little time adventure? Well, Zara was her grandmother. Just let me finish! Sylvia was the daughter of her son and everybody was very fond of her. But then they discovered that she was suffering from some incurable disease, that is, incurable in those times. They lost her, but they managed to arrange one last thing for her. Well, it was a long shot, but it gave her at least a chance to be revived and restored to health one day by greatly advanced future technology. You know that there was this trend that started in the twentieth and reached its peak in the mid twenty first century, *Cryonics,* or more comonly known - the Deep freeze..."

"Wait, I thought that the theory was discredited and..."

"It was, but not before a fair number of people went for it. It is illegal now, but that's neither here, nor there. Because there was an accident, an avalanche, or a flood or whatever and as a result the laboratory was destroyed, or so they thought, till it was discovered recently by archaeologists. They succeeded to revive two people only and one of them is my aunt."

Julian was willing to accompany Sophia to the Adapt Centre, but she decided it was better to go on her own. Later he met her at the heliterminal and led her towards his sleek custom-built slidercraft.

"Tell me, what happened, did you see her?" he asked immediately, when they had got into the craft.

Sophia smiled and he saw sparkles in her blue eyes.

"Let's go home and I'll tell you everything. I'm starving!"

This was a relief; he was rather apprehensive about this meeting. And such an extraordinary meeting it must've been. He wished he could've been there to witness it.

"She looks just fine," Sophia was saying, "and the doctors are very happy with her progress; she will make a full recovery. They want to keep her another week or two, just in case, but...of course she is very eager to see the new world, which is going to be her home from now on!"

"That's all very poetic, I am sure, but did you talk to her at all? Did you tell her who you are?"

"Of course I did. But she knew already. They've told her. Let's think lunch now! I like your vehicle, but I had a long journey and I would rather sit in the conservatory in front of a table!"

"I wanted to come with you...you didn't let me," protested Julian. "We could've stayed the night in Paris and could've had a wonderful meal there. I know this place..."

Sophia patted him affectionately on the shoulder:

"You don't want to admit that you couldn't contain your curiosity! Next time we could go together to collect her and we could stop at Paris too. Satisfied?"

They were having a big welcome dinner the first evening after Sylvia's arrival. It was an exciting event, especially for Sylvia who was enjoying every bit of it - trying new foods, asking hundreds of questions and just being glad to be alive. In a way she was given a second chance, she still hadn't got used to it and regarded it as a miracle, which most certainly it was.

Sophia and Julian got into the spirit of it too, there were jokes and laughter and even songs at the end. They looked at the girl, wondering at her high spirits and understood why she was such a favourite with the family. She wasn't exactly a beauty, but there was something very appealing about her, especially in the expression of her fine, dark eyes, sparkling under the heavy black lashes.

Time just disappeared imperceptibly that night. Eventually Sylvia had to go to bed, she was very tired and she was not supposed to overdo it for the moment. Sophia and Julian withdrew to the library for a glass of cognac. Sophia sat in her favourite armchair, hand on her forehead, while Julian was pouring the spirit. She seemed to be miles away again.

"You promised to tell me the story," Julian reminded her.

"Oh, that story! But you have to read it, to appreciate it fully. It is an unusual story, to be written by a young girl, what was she at the time? Twelve, I should think. You heard her saying, that her granny Zara helped her a little, but I bet, the idea was hers. Anyway, there is this alien, who comes to Earth, funny, it was before we managed to establish contact with the Vegeans, because he is very much like them, not physically of course. He does not understand the concept of violence or cruelty or murder; his race is unlike ours in that respect, they just don't have such things happening on their planet. He falls for this Earth woman, probably because she is so different, passionate and temperamental. And then there is that moment, which is so funny - she has a dentist, who comes to do some work on her teeth; the methods of the dentists haven't changed that much it seems, technology or not. I still dread the moment when I have an appointment with my dentist. So she sits in her chair with her mouth wide open, having the dentist poking into it with his instruments and at that moment here comes our alien, who decides that his girlfriend is being tortured, pushes the dentist away from her and badly injures him in the process, kneels in front of the girl and embraces her feet. Which just goes to show that even the most peaceful of species, can be provoked, where love is concerned. As for dentists, well, nobody likes them, not now, not then..."

"It's a great story, but I suspect, that another dental appointment is coming for you..."

"Well, if it is, I don't want to think about it yet. However, you should read the story, believe me, it's worth it."

"I will. As a bedtime story it will probably relax me," Julian promised.

"Really? You lucky man! Any mention of dentists would keep me fully awake for hours... I hope Sylvia will be able to sleep well. It is not the room, where she is used to sleep, but the other one really needs major work to be done to it, don't you think?"

"Don't worry, she'll be all right, after all those centuries in the ice..." Julian sipped some more of the golden liquid from his glass and added, "it was a good idea to give her the chance to make the plans and to design her own bedroom. It will save lots of money too..."

"Julian, be serious. We have a difficult task, I am saying "we", because I count on you, or shouldn't I? Well then, just think about it, we are supposed to bring up this teenager, who comes from a very different time, a time when there was a great division between the poor and the rich, a time when people held very different values..."

"What do you mean by different values?"

"Well, they were much more materialistic for a start," replied Sophia impatiently. "Yes, I know what you think – we both come from the same wealthy family, she should feel at home here, in our old ancestral house but still it's not an easy task we are undertaking. We have to help her find her place in society, make society accept her."

Julian was shaking his head:

"Society will accept her all right, she is young, she is charming, she is unique. She has memories of times long past, would be sought after by writers, historians like yourself, anthropologists, sociologists. Will have more opportunities than most. And most certainly will be pestered by the press," he predicted.

"The press doesn't know her whereabouts. At least for now. Information is not released easily from the Adapt Centre and they will keep it that way, till they find out everything worth knowing about her. The other person, who was discovered, would have a lot more problems, I dare say. He is 31 and he is of royal blood, a prince. So you see..."

"A prince! You didn't tell me that. What's his name?"

"I haven't got a clue. That is all I know. I could find out, if you are so curious. I just didn't have the chance to inquire. With Sylvia coming and all..."

"A prince! So now it's really becoming like a fairy tale. Life doesn't stop to amaze me. First Sylvia, now this prince, the story of the Sleeping beauty, isn't it?"

Sophia stretched and stifled a yawn:

"In this day and age, there should be things to fire our imagination. Otherwise life would be very boring, indeed. But I am tired, it's getting late."

"Wait, wait, have another glass and let's dream on a little longer. What if..."

At last Sylvia's room was ready and she moved in. She was pleased with the result, though it could never be what it once was. Nevertheless, she was at home, the only home, she had ever had and although considerably altered, it still remained "Elounda", the house her Granddad had once built for his family, the place where she had been brought up and lived all her previous life, that is up to the Deep Freeze period. A home is like an anchor, she thought and pleased with this analogy repeated it to herself:

"An anchor."

One needed an anchor in this ever changing world. Everything else had changed, but "Elounda" was still there, it had waited for her all this time to shelter her on her return.

Sylvia started to arrange some of her old books, she had discovered, while rummaging round the place. Real books were rare and these, considering their age, were very expensive too, so she was proud with her find. She had also discovered her little robot. Robots were fashionable in the mid to late 21st century and almost every family had one. They could do simple household tasks, keep the children company and in general act as mechanical pets. There were few modifications to be made to Sylvia's robot, before she could use him again, but like his mistress, time had obviously been merciful to him.

For the moment everybody was gradually settling into a routine, Sylvia had become part of it and things were generally looking good. She had a lot to tell about her family and life in her century in general. Sometimes she would feel nostalgic about it and would cry a little, but every teenager has their mood swings, so it was nothing out of the ordinary. But then one day she had to go to the Adapt Centre for some more tests and she met the prince.

As Sophia was telling Julian later, she knew something like that was coming. They felt drawn to each other right away. Undeniably, being so to speak contemporaries, they had so much more in common than with anybody else. Regular communications were established between them and Sylvia was talking about her prince all the time.

"He is not suitable for her," Sophia was saying to Julian one afternoon, watching Sylvia and her robot, playing in the garden. "She should be making friends with somebody of her own age group."

"You are becoming like a mother hen. It's interesting to see you lecturing your great-great aunt on her relationships. I told you Prince Charming was coming, but you wouldn't listen."

"I don't believe in love at first sight," Sophia objected, "she hardly knows him. Love, the way I see it, blossoms gradually."

Julian looked her straight in the eye:

"Are you telling me that you've never ever been shot by Cupid's arrow all of a sudden?"

Blushing, she lowered her eyes under his eloquent gaze. Julian smiled contentedly.

"I wouldn't worry, if I were you," he added. "Sylvia is not stupid, she will do what's best for her and it's not for us to meddle, like it or not. Everybody has their own life to live."

"Probably you are right, but still, it weights heavily on my mind. Do you know, she soaks like a sponge everything he says and even comes up with some of his expressions at times, something that considering her age, I find really disconcerting."

"Such as?" Julian inquired, curious.

"Such as: 'Anachronisms like us should stick together!' That's what I was told when I gently remonstrated with her while she was about to call him instead of concentrating on her studies."

Sylvia dashed in, enveloped by a gust of wind, rubbing her hands; her cheeks were flushed but she was smiling at them:

"It's cold out there, isn't it? In the 21st we had warmer autumns, more sunshine. But then they were all talking about the global warming. What happened with all that? It seems they were wrong, were they not? Or was it because you stopped using petrol as a fuel?"

She was trying in vain to smooth her unruly hair, dishevelled by the wind.

"Not entirely, no," replied Sophia, "it had more to do with the sun's activities. Certainly using other energy sources improved things, but as you can see we still haven't got the balance right. It's too cold. So how is the robot?"

She looked at the little metal automaton, who had followed Sylvia unhurriedly, unperturbed by the forces of nature.

"Oh Sophie, call him Stuart, it's his name and he responds to it, don't you, Stuart?"

The robot rolled on his wheels to face her and answered:

"I am Stuart."

"Oh I am sure you are," said Sophia. "What lessons did Sylvia have today?"

"No lessons. Today is a holiday," duly answered the robot.

"A holiday? What holiday is that?"

"It's Halloween. Don't you celebrate it anymore?" exclaimed Sylvia. "It's hardly a surprise, it seems you have forgotten how to celebrate, how to have fun."

"Halloween. I know," said Julian, "people dress up and go around like spectres, phantoms, witches and the like. What a horrible idea. I certainly wouldn't have fun, doing that. And I am surprised, that someone like you would like it either. As for fun, I think we could have our share of fun, doing something more useful. I am planning to go to Sofia for another 'back in time' experience. You could come with me, if you think it would be fun."

"Julian! Is it going to happen there this time? Why haven't you told me?" exclaimed Sophia.

"To see you burning with curiosity, of course. No, the truth is, there is nothing final yet. I need to run more tests. I could've gone to a couple of other places of course, where such occurrences took place, but the time was not convenient, besides, this is where you wanted to go all along."

"What are you two talking about?" asked Sylvia. "We were discussing Halloween and then..."

Julian shook his head with a mischievous smile:

"Oh it's a long story. But I promise you a lot of fun. It's very exciting. Let's dress for dinner now, look what time it is!"

Left on his own in the drawing room Julian turned to the robot:

"It's just you and me, old friend. Do you know where Sofia is?"

A few grunts came out of the robot, before he answered:

"Sofia. The capital of the Bulgarians, situated on the Balkan Peninsula."

"Right. What a clever little fellow you are. I wonder what else you have got on your chips."

"Sofia was founded by the Thracians in antiquity. Unsurprisingly its motto states: "It grows but it does not age". In Roman times it was called Serdica, in Byzantine times – Triaditsa, in medieval times - Sredets, by the Slavs, and eventually Sofia, taking the name from the ancient church St. Sofia, which still stands in the city centre."

"Wow, that's impressive. Shall we take you with us? You could act as a guide. In any event, if my experiment doesn't work, at least we could do some sightseeing, couldn't we?"

TO VENTURE INTO THE FUTURE

Sylvia examined critically her image reflected in the mirror and made a face:

"What were those fashion designers thinking of to come up with such a creation? I hate this dress! OK, hate is probably too strong, but let's say, I've taken a dislike to it."

Sophia shrugged her shoulders with exasperation:

"What do you expect? Times have changed. That's what we wear today. You have to get used to the new trends."

"But I don't like it. It is absolutely grotesque. Look at those shoulders! Don't I look ridiculous?"

She turned and looked at her profile scowling, hands on her hips. Sophia smiled remembering the time when a teenager herself, she was no less self-conscious with similar misgivings when looking in a mirror. Now sitting on Sylvia's bed in the girl's bedroom and surveying abstractedly the elegant but rather dated decor, she felt quite detached as if it wasn't her she was seeing in her mind's eye.

"I must be getting older," she reflected, "how time flies! Is it really Sylvia there in front of that glass, or a younger me experiencing the same frustrations?"

In the mirror her eyes met Sylvia's pleading ones:

"Why don't we go to a shop or a dressmaker or somewhere where I can try something different?" asked the girl tossing her unruly hair.

"My dear, the nearest dressmaker is miles from here. And it costs a fortune to have designer clothes. But we can see a pretty good selection on line and order whatever you want."

"Now you are talking! Let's go."

But Sophia didn't budge from her comfortable position:

"We don't have to go anywhere. Look, there's your computer terminal, we'll just make use of one or more of the screens. All you need to do is to ask Jeeves."

"Jeeves?" Sylvia giggled. "The butler, you mean? Or was he someone's valet? You know, the main character from that book, what was the title again? It slipped my mind."

"I don't know about that book; what I can tell you is that in old times, at the dawn of EIN, there was a search engine, called by that name."

"What is EIN?" Sylvia asked baffled.

"But you should know this by now, my dear girl! Haven't they taught you anything at the Adapt Centre? EIN is an abbreviation for the Earth's Info-Net, I think you must know it as the Internet."

"The Internet, of course! They did tell me that, but there is so much to remember! My head is bursting. Give me a break, Sophie!"

"Sorry, my dear! I keep forgetting what a journey you've been on. But let's proceed. Nowadays we use the name Jeeves for our home computers."

Sophia motioned vaguely towards the screen:

"Jeeves! We want the new autumn collection. Here it is. You probably don't care to see those pretentious girls doing the modelling, but rather yourself wearing the outfits and decide if you like any of them. Let's access your scans done already at the Adapt centre and use them. There! That'll do it. All your measurements are here. Now it's all set and we can start our own fashion show."

On the big screen appeared Sylvia's 3D image absolutely naked, walking somewhat unnaturally towards them in a robotic fashion.

"Wow! That's impressive!" exclaimed the real Sylvia. "Although I don't think I walk quite like that, do I?"

"No, but that's not important. Of course we can fiddle with it a bit more to get it right, but it would take time. You just want to have the overall idea how the clothes will fit."

"What do we do now?"

"You have to choose a dress and try it."

"Let's see. What about this one?"

"Number three. Fine. Now choose the colour."

"Let's go for the floral pattern – number 7."

The next moment Sylvia's image was walking towards them wearing the floral dress. It then turned away so they were able to see it from behind. They looked at it from every possible angle and even saw the effect if blown by the wind or walking above a ventilation shaft, not unlike Marilyn Monroe in her famous scene.

Having seen how it worked, Sylvia found it easy to use the program and got totally engrossed in it, trying different styles and different patterns and colour schemes. Sophia left her to it for she had other work to do.

Later she found Julian sitting in the library, jotting some notes in his E-pad. There was no sign of Sylvia and Julian hadn't seen her the whole afternoon. They wondered what she was up to. It wasn't for long. Sylvia ran into the room, her eyes sparkling and started telling them about the clothes she'd ordered and how she'd found some fabulous bedding, so she immediately thought that it would be nice to have everything in her bedroom colour coordinated – from the duvet covers and curtains to the matching towels, dressing gown and slippers. She stopped her tirade when she saw that Julian couldn't suppress his laughter:

"You think it's a bit over the top don't you?"

"Yes, you don't want to overdo it, do you? You'll soon start hating those colours if you see them splashed everywhere around you and have to start all over again, don't you think?"

"I suppose I overdid it, didn't I? Can I cancel some of those items?"

"Of course you can," replied Julian, "but let's have dinner first, it's getting late."

"Do you order everything on line, Julian, or do you go to the shops?"

"Yes, you can go to the shops, but they are usually more expensive, so most people prefer to do it on line. And it's more convenient."

"We had shopping on line already in my time," said Sylvia thoughtfully, "but some didn't like it. My auntie Charlotte used to say that it alienated people. I went to the supermarket with her one day during our stay in England. They had recently introduced those super-duper tills in their shop, where you scan the items yourself. I thought it was fun, we didn't have it in France yet, not here at any rate. Auntie said she wasn't keen on it. Before that she always used to have a chat with the shop assistants, but since the new tills were introduced, they started to get rid of the staff and those who stayed were so busy dealing with old ladies and the like who had trouble to work the self service devices, that they didn't have any time left to speak to the other customers."

"Well, it was probably more efficient that way," remarked Julian.

"It was. I personally liked it. But my auntie Charlotte was lonely. And she was chatty too. Perhaps a bit overbearing, but otherwise nice. Her husband was travelling a lot. He was a salesman. And her son, well, he was about my age, just a bit older and had his friends. She complained that he was hardly ever there. Mind you, *I* saw a lot of him during our visit."

"He didn't fancy you, did he?"

"I don't think so. We got on. Jamie was really nice. But I fancied his friend Bill. He was good looking. I went out with them a lot. They showed me around. We had such a terrific time! We walked along the Thames and took a boat trip and visited Windsor Castle and saw Magna Carta monument. We walked into the fields and there was so much wild life there; a lot more than at home in France: birds, squirrels and rabbits and even a deer, which was actually a doe for it was followed by a fawn."

42

Julian was listening to her with an amused expression on his face. He was born precisely in the area Sylvia was describing, but a lot later of course. It was weird to listen to this young girl, young enough to be his daughter, to be talking about her life in a time when even his parents were not born yet. Sylvia in meantime was still pursuing her story down memory lane, not concerned at all if someone was listening or not:

"The following day I sneaked out to meet Bill. He rang me and told me where to find him. I went to the field and spotted a sign: someone had been spreading flour on the grass, forming an arrow, then another one and so on. I followed them till I got to a secret spot under the trees where Bill was waiting for me.

Only the birds were there to witness our first kiss; it was heaven. I remember lying in the grass that summer night and smoking a cigarette; we were not allowed to smoke of course being minors, besides there was a cigarette ban and all, but the boys had smuggled some cigarettes from somewhere and a few cans of beer and we had our little party there in the grass. The sunset was absolutely fabulous, colouring the sky and the clouds in all shades of red and purple; later the first moon appeared and we listened to the song of the crickets."

"I will feel homesick if you carry on like that," said Julian at this point, "I haven't been back there for awhile and there are still places left like that field you were just talking about."

"Yes, let's talk about something else. They, my friends I mean, are all gone now and I find this difficult to accept."

She sighed. Her mind kept wondering towards those last days in her own time, just before the Deep Freeze. Those were sad memories. She saw herself as a tragic figure, a modern Juliet going to an early grave and hoping to see her beloved, one last time. But it wasn't meant to be. Her Romeo, Bill was hundreds of miles away, in Britain, while she was languishing in the South of France. There was no way he could come over to see her just like that. They spoke

43

often of course. He would ring her every evening, confused, embarrassed, lost for words. She could see his face on the screen of her mobile, she would try to sound brave and composed, but usually would fail miserably. Bill's attempts to cheer her up didn't work either. She couldn't care less for the football matches, he was so enthusiastic about, neither was she that bothered about the latest gadgets he got for his birthday. Poor Bill! Searching the archives, she had found out that he had joined the army and had been killed in some foreign land quite early on. Poor, poor Bill! She sighed again and turned to Julian, making an effort to pull herself together:

"But tell me about England, Julian. They told me at the Adapt centre that the political borders have become rather meaningless, the old countries are no more, or at least not what they once were. What exactly did they mean? I am not with it. I remember Gran saying once that borders don't make much sense and I found this a strange notion. How is that possible? What about governments?"

"I think that Sophie will explain this better than me. She is a historian after all."

Sophia helped herself to some more salad before replying:

"We have economic regions now. It works much better and it makes more sense, because each region has a local governing body which looks after the common interests. The big countries of the past, like France for example, consisted of a number of regions quite different geographically and economically.

A new trend started towards the end of the first century of the second millennium where neighbouring areas with similar conditions started developing a joint infrastructure together and mutual interdependence. Take this area where we live for example: it is part of France politically, but France as a country has long since lost its significance. We are now in the so called Maritime Alps consisting of what was formerly just a departement of France coupled with the Ligurian coastal area of Italy.

The north is still the more industrialised part of Europe as it always has been and the south has become even more touristy than formally. But it has to compete with the Middle East of course."

"But the Middle East was just a war zone in my time," interjected Sylvia. "How did they proceed with the peace process there? It looked absolutely hopeless at the time."

"Well, it was hopeless," agreed Sophia. "But when the oil industry lost its importance, the interest shifted elsewhere and that part of the world had to re-establish peaceful relations and make a new start. A regeneration process took place and once things got back to normal, the tourist industry began to flourish too, which is not surprising for a land so rich in history."

"But if the oil industry declined, that means that you've found new energy sources."

"We had to. Oil was becoming too expensive and eventually the Clean Coal Technology lobby prevailed," intervened Julian.

"Coal? You can't be serious! I was taught at school…"

Julian was dismissive:

"Never mind what you were taught at school! This technology existed long before it was actually introduced commercially, it was already there when you were around, I am sure. The idea is truly ingenious, believe you me! Various processes had been designed to remove or intercept CO_2 from coal and store it underground; and then a technique had been devised of converting unworked coal deep underground into a combustible gas which, using this Clean Coal Technology, contains no CO_2. So that's how we obtained clean energy with minimum greenhouse emissions. Later we started mining the Moon."

"That's true," pursued Sophia. "It was discovered that the moon is rich in titanium and helium. Since the moment

China joined the space race in a bid to start exploiting the lunar mineral resources, things started to move really quickly. The rest of the world didn't want to be left behind and so the Helium rush started. The importance of helium lies in the fact that it can be used as an efficient fuel for the nuclear fusion reactors that were under development at the time. So the stakes were high indeed and it didn't go without bloodshed. But after the initial chaos and confusion, things started to settle down. The lunar colonies have now gained their autonomy and despite the fact that they depend to a large extent on Earth's good will for life sustaining supplies, they stand their ground and defend their own."

"But surely those interests coincide?" countered Sylvia.

"You would be surprised how much your viewpoint alters with changes in circumstances. Believe you me, I know it from experience," Sophia shook her head emphatically.

"How do you mean?"

"My parents live and work on the Moon or shall I say in the Moon because it's all underground."

"Your parents! I didn't know they were alive!" exclaimed Sylvia. "You never talk about them."

"There is not much to talk about. We don't get on. It's as simple as that. They left when I was young to join in the family business there. It was actually your brother's son who started it all, the first of us to become a prospector on the Moon. My parents are scientists and are highly valued there. With time they've become so involved in their research, which they consider extremely important, that it seems that nothing else matters for them. But then again my views might be coloured, I might just be unfair. As I said, it all depends on the viewpoint,"

"But don't you meet when they come back home?"

"Home? Their home is up there on the Moon. They are not coming back. Ever," Sophia sounded resigned to the fact.

"Never? But why?"

"Why? For a start it's the Earth's gravitation that they can't get re-accustomed to. They've been away for far too long. People who come back to Earth after being on the Moon for many years feel very uncomfortable here and find it very hard, if not impossible, to re-adjust. Usually they don't remain long. Besides, there is nothing here for my parents, they don't fit in, they don't even belong to this place any more. This house means everything to me, but they don't care about it at all. Father actually left it for my use; they are happy with what they've got on the Moon."

"Don't you ever talk to them?" Sylvia asked.

"Oh yes. We talk every now and then."

"Can I talk to them?"

"My dear Sylvie, what the devil for?" Sophia exclaimed.

"Why not? Haven't you told them about me?"

"Of course I have. They took it in their stride," Sophia smiled, recalling the conversation she had had, "asked me if you are anything like your renowned nephew whose holographic image takes a prominent place on their walk of Fame. I said there seems to be some family resemblance. They were pleased. They said I should take good care of you."

"That's nice. I would love to talk to them directly. Can I? Please!"

Sophia hesitated. She looked towards Julian who'd been silent throughout the whole conversation. He imperceptibly shrugged his shoulders. But Sylvia noticed it. She rolled her eyes up. Sophia gave in:

"Well, if you insist. But not right now. All in good time."

"Tomorrow then," persisted Sylvia.

"Young people today, so impetuous!" said Julian with a grin. "You have to promise her, Sophie, otherwise she won't leave us finish our meal."

"I will," countered Sylvia, "for I intend to turn in now. I'm quite sleepy. You don't mind, do you?"

And without waiting for a reply, she ran out of the room. Julian chuckled and shook his head:

"Young people!"

"There it is! Look!"

Sophia was pointing towards the screen. It was later that evening and she had retired to the library followed shortly by Julian as was their custom. He looked at the photo of the middle aged man with auburn hair slightly grey at the temples; his dark blue eyes were a bit sad but there was also the hint of an ironic smile illuminating his features.

"So this is him?" asked Julian.

"Yes. James Osborn," Sophia looked pleased, "Sylvia's cousin. You see, he became a successful writer."

"No doubt inspired by his grandmother," Julian remarked.

"No doubt," Sophia agreed readily, "it runs in the family. He left us mainly fiction but also his memoirs. I hadn't read it before, but as Sylvia mentioned him, I thought, I'd better have a look. And there it is. I'll need some time to go through it, of course because as you might expect it's rather long. It was published in three volumes at the time. But I've marked this extract:"

JAMIE'S MEMOIRS

("Elounda" Archive)

Summer 202x

Sweet little Sylvia. I can still see her in front of me, as if it was yesterday and not all those years ago. For one so full of life, who would've thought it would end up like that? I felt fate was rather cruel when I heard what had happened to her.

But now, today I don't want to think about that. I haven't reached that part of my story yet. We are still in the summer of 202x when we are young and life seems to offer us unlimited opportunities, we all feel as if we are on top of the world.

It's twilight when I set off for the field to find Sylvia and Bill. Finding them is not going to be much of a problem, because it was I who organised this clandestine meeting of theirs in the first instance. I don't know why I agreed to help them out. Frankly I don't understand at all what she sees in him. All right, he's my mate, I shouldn't talk like that about him, but still – the truth is that he's a jerk. He didn't even have a clue how to go about things, so he came to me for advice on how to date a girl like Sylvie: "She's your cousin, pal, you know her better." I hardly knew her at all. When was the last time that I've set eyes on her before now? We must've been still in the kindergarten stage. Anyhow! I explained to him that most teenage girls are quite romantic; they go for the mushy stuff, so he better come up with something along those lines. But was that enough of a hint for my clueless friend? Nah. He needs to be led every step of the way: "If I get her a bunch of flowers, I'd look rather silly, won't I?" Yeah, I can just imagine it.

So I put my brains to work and came up with this pretty original idea involving spreading flour around in the shape of arrows to lead Sylvia into the field for a private interview with our Bill. That appeals to him, so we put it in motion. I am to join them later, after giving them enough time to talk, but knowing how articulate Bill is, I now wonder if I shouldn't have interrupted them earlier.

Anyway I follow the path, trying to avoid the dog shit, which is all over the place among the flour arrows. Sylvia says that I should've seen the streets of Nice before complaining about our path, but I am a bit dubious, that French pooches would leave so fertile a trail as our local canines.

I climb a stile, have a look to check if there is anyone around and go into the undergrowth, making as much noise as possible to warn lover boy and his date that I'm coming. Finally I arrive at the spot and there they are: Sylvia looks as pleased as the cat that got the cream and Bill, hmm, Bill looks a tiny bit on edge.

I take the rugsack off my back and shove it in Bill's hands, while I demonstratively place my arm round Sylvia's waist, saying:

"That's enough snogging for today, my dear. Let's go and have a drink and a ciggy."

She smiles but she's not the least embarrassed. We head out into the open and I lead the way to the other field where the farmer has been round with his tractor today and has left behind (very conveniently) a number of well packed hay bales, ready for collection in a day or two, but right now the venue for our little party tonight.

Sylvia is thrilled. She runs towards a bale and climbs on top of it. We follow her unhurriedly, "a gentleman should never run" as they say. Bill and I settle at the base of the bale. He rummages in the rugsack and produces cans of beer and ciggies that I have obtained after much contrivance. I open one for Sylvia and hand it up to her.

"Perfect," she murmurs, taking a big sip.

Suddenly she leans towards me and kisses me on the cheek:

"Thanks, Jamie, you are a sweetie."

I am not so sure I want to be "a sweetie", but I don't mind her kiss. At least one of them should show some gratitude towards me for organising such a perfect date. Then I realise that she is not supposed to know I am involved. But perhaps she suspects it. Come on, Sylvie, can you really believe that Bill can come up with something like that? No way, no bloody way.

Sylvia lies on her back and smokes, looking at the sky. There are planes flying above us, because the airport is so close, but we can't hear them, due to the noise coming from the traffic on the nearby road. It gets worse and worse these days, it seems people don't get out of their cars at all. This wouldn't have bothered me that much if I wasn't going for my driving licence; that is I am due to start my driving lessons next year, but I hear that they are making the test more difficult for new drivers, trying to dissuade them or something to make them "better road users". Yeah, right. I just have to have that driving licence, no matter what; you can't manage without one in this day and age.

It's dark now and we are able to see the stars. I can recognise the Big Dipper and point it out to Sylvia. We start talking about space exploration; are they really going for that colony on the Moon? It takes them a hell of a lot of time to organise it. They are now about to start work on the far side, I inform Sylvia, where rich deposits of helium and titanium are to be found. She asks what about a breathable atmosphere and I reply, that's not a problem, there is a mineral, ilmenite, that can be used to generate the oxygen needed for the human habitat.

Bill can't contribute anything to the conversation. Astronomy is not really his thing. But he seems happy enough with his beer; I just want to wipe that stupid smirk off his face, but I can't possibly do it in Sylvia's presence. It's getting late. We have to go before we are assaulted by mobile phone calls from parents, saying it's well past our bedtime.

End of selected extract

Sophia looked at Julian:
"So, what do you think?"
"Fascinating read!"

"It is, isn't it? I like his style, I must say. But it's absolutely unbelievable what those kids were getting up to."

"You sound shocked. Come on, Sophie, don't tell me you haven't been in for similar escapades when you were their age."

"To tell you the truth, I haven't," she paused, before resuming. "Mind you, I have been rather naughty at times but it just wasn't the same. For a start I was rather shy and did not have that many friends; nothing like it. The ones I had were of a different breed altogether – prim and proper and wouldn't do anything their parents won't approve. More to the point, smoking was more or less eradicated at the time, beer was not particularly popular and drinking in general wasn't seen in anyway as the forbidden fruit. I was offered the odd glass of wine at home when we had dinner parties and nobody thought much of it."

Julian tried hard to imagine Sophie being a mischievous little thing, but he couldn't. She was so dainty and coy. People don't change as much as that. Or do they?

"You took it too literally, Sophie. I didn't mean smoking or drinking per se. I had myself only the vaguest notions what cigarette smoking was like, for it was eradicated even earlier in England, about the time this memoir of Jamie's was published. What I meant was the whole little episode, especially because we've heard about it from Sylvia, before coming across Jamie's version."

"Yes. The point of view of a teenage boy as opposed to a girl's point of view," added Sophia.

Julian grinned:

"Which one scores then?"

"I can't say. They are just different, that's all. But shall I show it to Sylvia?"

"Good question," he thought of the expression on Sylvia s face when she was recounting the story. "Somehow I don't think it's such a great idea. It will be amusing to see her reaction, but on the other hand she might get upset."

Sophia readily agreed:

"You are right as usual. Perhaps I'll do it at a later stage, when I feel the moment is right."

She smiled at Julian:

"Tired?"

"Rather. It's been a long day. But I am progressing, you know. Things are looking promising and we might be going to Sofia, as I hoped. But I have some more work to get through before that."

Sylvia was sitting comfortably in Sophia's chair leaning over her desk. The screen on the wall was flickering and she waited patiently for it to clear.

"Sorry," Sophia said, "it's not ideal, but again interplanetary connections never are. It's better now, isn't it?"

An elderly lady dressed in an outlandish outfit was smiling at them from the monitor.

"Hello, Mrs. Leonard," said Sylvia.

"Hello, my child. Hello, Sophie dear. It's so strange to hear somebody calling me Mrs. Leonard. My name is Saskia," she smiled again, a calm, serene smile.

Sylvia couldn't see any family resemblance between mother and daughter. But then the father appeared on the screen, waving his hand and she knew who Sophia had taken after.

"We wanted to show you something, Sylvia," he said, reaching for an object out of her line of vision. "There!" he exclaimed triumphantly, holding up a little statue made of some shiny metal.

"It's a statuette," Sylvia said puzzled.

"Not any old statuette, mind. This is your illustrious nephew, and you should be real proud of him."

He brandished the figurine excitedly. Sylvia looked at it but couldn't distinguish its features.

"Sure," replied Sylvia diplomatically, "sadly I didn't have the chance to meet him."

It was strange to have had a nephew, let alone a famous one. And how come a brat like her brother Matt should produce such an offspring?

"Oh well," the old gent didn't quite know what to say, but his wife added quickly:

"But happily we have been lucky to meet you! We wanted to invite you to come and live with us on the Moon, if you were willing of course. I don't understand why we were not approached in the first instance. We learnt about your existence from Sophie, the Adapt Centre kept us in the dark and I am not impressed with them at all. The fact that we've left the Earth is neither here, nor there."

"Mother!"

"Don't interfere, Sophie. One would think we live on another planet."

"But you do live on another planet!"

"Sophie dear, you of all people should know better. The Moon is not another planet. It's a celestial body, yes. But otherwise it's just Earth's one and only natural satellite!"

"I am not going to argue the finer points of astronomy with you, mother."

"Of course not. Anyway, I just want Sylvia to know that it's not because of lack of hospitality on our side that she is not with us today. By rights she should've been brought to us. But Sylvia is old enough to make up her mind without being influenced by others. You are a part of the family, Sylvia. The invitation stands and if you wish, my dear, we'll arrange transport for you in no time."

Sophia rolled her eyes up but resisted the urge to have another outburst. She had the greatest opinion for Sylvia's social skills and trusted she'd handle the situation a lot better if just left to get on with it. She was not mistaken. Suppressing a smile she watched Sylvia with increasing admiration as the girl was profusely thanking Sophia's parents and promising them to think it over and to let them know if she decided to join them. At the same time she emphasised that she was happy where she was and Sophia was very nice to her, oh yes, they did get on perfectly well and they would miss each other if she decided to leave. At last when the final good byes were said and the familiar faces had finally disappeared from the screen, Sophia sighed with relief.

IT GROWS BUT IT DOES NOT AGE

The view was that of an old church, preserved as if by a miracle all these centuries and they could not take their eyes off it. It was unbelievable how merciful time had been to it; wars, natural disasters and human interference had spared it and there it was – a stylish and elegant basilica in the shape of a cross with red brick walls; an oasis of peace in the middle of a huge and busy Metropolis.

Julian had to wait for the right time for his long planned experiment, so they used the opportunity to see the city where one of Sophia's and Sylvia's ancestors came from. Now they stood enchanted and fascinated, staring out of a hotel window at this amazing church. Sylvia was the first to break the silence; only fifteen yet having behind her centuries in the Deep Freeze, she was impatient to discover this new world, full of mysteries:

"Shouldn't we go there, instead of looking like that? Come on, guys!"

And then the communicator rang and flashed, someone was trying to get in touch with them.

"It's probably the hotel administration, nobody else knows we are here," said Julian.

But he was wrong. When he activated it, the huge screen lit up showing a smiling face – it was the face of Prince Adrian, Sylvia's friend.

"Hello there! You've turned up eventually! It's been two days now since I've arrived here and believe me, I had a rather exciting time, seeing all these churches and ancient ruins! I am looking forward to showing you round…"

"What on earth are you doing here?" Julian was not very polite; he was taken aback by the unexpected encounter.

"But, my dear chap, I am taking part in your little expedition! Hasn't Sylvia told you yet? Haven't you Sylvia?"

Cornered, Sylvia had to admit that indeed she had invited the prince, but hadn't dared to tell them out of fear that they would be against her little scheme. And she was right about it, of course. After abruptly ending the conversation, Sophia turned towards Sylvia, ready for a confrontation:

"What on earth did you think you were doing?"

Julian waved his hand partly as a sign of resignation, partly to pacify the two women. And then Sylvia said:

"You don't have the right to tell me what to do. You are not my parents, nor my guardians. Adrian is my guardian for now, it's all sorted out! Till my coming of age; then we'll get married. It makes perfect sense to both of us. If you don't like it – *tant pis*, as Adrian says, you cannot please everybody!"

There was a silence, as if a bomb had fallen. Then Sophia turned and left the room. Julian wondered what he was supposed to do. Run after Sophia to comfort her, argue the point with Sylvia or just go to sort out his own affairs…a difficult choice.

"Look, Sylvia, that's not how a family functions. We discuss our problems, we think things over, we compromise sometimes… We've become a family – you, Sophia and me. And when one of us doesn't take the others into consideration, it really hurts. Please, think about this!"

An hour or so later, after lots of tears and apologies, "I'll never ever do it again"-s and the rest of it, the trio was out in the street, still shaken by the events and somewhat subdued, on its way to meet the prince.

Adrian was sitting in an open air café opposite the ancient theatre building and talking to his dog (he never went anywhere without him); a beautiful Irish setter, the same breed as the one he had had before the period of the Deep Freeze; quite a rare breed these days, when hunting was more or less extinct. The dog, called Rufus, was provided with a fashionable collar equipped with a special gadget, picking up on the canine emotions and translating them into an approximate yet comprehensible human speech. How well that worked, was anybody's guess. The majority of dog owners were very impressed and pleased to be able to communicate with their pets. The little transmitter announced: "I am delighted" and so he was; anybody could see that!

The prince brightened when he saw our little party coming towards him. He was eager to tell them how well he'd spent his time, waiting for them, how much he'd enjoyed being there, how willing he was to be their guide, having already seen the main sights of the metropolis…To their surprise Julian and Sophia got on quite well with him.

Before long they were all moving in the direction of the basilica they had admired earlier from their hotel window. It was built in Byzantine times and had given its name to the city itself. It was cool and dimly lit inside, the smell of incense flooding the nostrils. Each of them lit a candle and placed it in one of the brass candelabra in front of the iconostasis. Adrian motioned towards the right and they followed obediently in single file. He pressed a button and suddenly an old book appeared in front of their eyes.

"A hologram!" whispered Julian.

"A hologram!" echoed Sylvia.

"It's been commissioned in medieval times by a king and made by a monk," explained Adrian in a whisper.

"It's one of the Gospels," remarked Sophia, looking attentively at the cover.

Adrian pressed the button again to start a slide show. Page after page was unveiled before them showing an array of beautiful pictures accompanying the text.

"This is the Royal family. They say it is a real likeness of the king who commissioned the work. He must've been quite arrogant to have his portrait depicted on a page of the Holy book," remarked Adrian.

"What do you expect? God's representative on Earth," replied Julian. "I've seen a medieval Bible showing David but as the spitting image of King Henry VIII!"

"Ah, that one! He was arrogant all right!" observed Sophia.

Sylvia wasn't listening. She was obviously fascinated by the ancient book. Suddenly she exclaimed:

"Look! He's talking to the Virgin Mary here. I remember now, he is called Tsar Ivan Alexander and I've seen the original of this book!"

"Keep your voice down, child!" whispered Sophia, "this is a church after all!"

"Sorry! It was so unexpected," whispered back Sylvia.

"You must tell us all about it when we go outside."

Typically impetuous for her 15 years, Sylvia, bursting to tell them all, finally had the opportunity to relate her story.

"It was when we were in England with Gran," she began.

"When did you go there?" asked Sophia.

"Some years ago, when I was young."

"They call it the La Manche Region now," observed Adrian.

"Yes, but back home, we still call it England!" replied Julian, "I regard myself as being first and foremost English."

"Are you going to listen to my story or not?" asked Sylvia impatiently. "And so while we were there, my Gran took me to an exhibition in London. There were lots of holy books on display, but she wanted to see this particular one, because it came from her country and also because it was the only one written in the Slavonic language. We were sorely disappointed though. First we had to wait for the library where the exhibition was, to open its wrought iron gate and let us in, to what was an uninspiring factory like building with pagoda elements, then go through security as if we were some bandits, though Gran said that "better safe than sorry, with all those terrorists about, one never knows," and eventually to see all those books placed in glass cases! Gran said that they were very precious, but we should've been able to see them online or something. The only page that we had the chance to see, was exactly the one with the picture of the Tsar himself, talking to the Virgin Mary. So now you know."

"Wow! You have been around quite a bit then, haven't you? We thought you had led a sheltered life," said Julian.

"Don't mind him, Sylvia," Sophia interrupted him, "you have to tell me more about your Gran, but we have to go now and finish our sightseeing tour."

So they walked around the centre, marvelled at the ruins, so well preserved and successfully incorporated into the modern urban landscape, discussing their plans as they went along. Julian had to do some more calculations and determine the most appropriate spot for their observations, while Sophia had some more research to do on the family history and Sylvia was due to help her there; so they were both going the next day to the Local Municipal Archives to look into some very old files, unavailable on EIN (the Earth's Info-Net).

"Being a historian gives you certain privileges," Sophia said lightly.

The next couple of days everybody was busy; even the prince. He volunteered to organise their free time and apparently was not going to spare any effort into keeping them entertained. Clearly he wanted to be in the good books of his new relations.

"You don't mind old Rip planning your free time, do you?" he asked lightly, "it will be a pleasure for me to do something useful; I've been out of action for so long."

"Who is Rip?" Julian was bemused.

Sylvia burst out laughing:

"Don't you know the story of Rip Van Winkle, Julian? He fell asleep under a tree and woke years later…"

Julian chuckled:

"Good Heavens! First we had Sleeping Beauty, now comes Rip Van Winkle! What next?"

Sylvia replied in the same style:

"The Time-traveller, of course and then Alice in wonderland! I don't need to mention any names, do I?"

"What a motley crew we make!" Adrian observed amused.

Sylvia raised her hands in excitement:

"Super! Adventures, here we come!"

It was early March and the weather was not yet very warm, but nice and sunny never the less. On the first Sunday they went to Vitosha, the mountain in the foothills of which Sofia is situated. The prince rented a little antigrav vehicle to take them to a very pretty spot with a superb view of the town. Pursuing their excursion they reached another site, also well worth seeing. It was a mountain river strewn with huge oval boulders that gave the impression of having been frozen in a moment of time while spilling over down the slope.

"This is what I call a natural phenomenon," explained Adrian proudly as if he had created this impressive stone river. "Apparently an ancient glacier, but what I wish to know is why do they refer to it as the Golden Bridges? They are neither golden, neither bridges. Does anybody know?" he looked at them enquiringly.

Nobody knew of course, neither did Adrian himself, but it didn't matter. It was time for lunch but Adrian had thought about this too. He had brought along a picnic basket and a folding table and chairs, museum exhibits that had been taken on loan. After lunch Rufus urged them to go for a walk. He was very excited and you did not need to hear all the exclamations of his little doggy transmitter!

His enthusiasm was irresistible, so they followed him away from the beaten track and into the woods; and this is where they had their little accident. Sylvia was distracted by some wild flowers and as a result did not look carefully where she was going; the next thing she knew she was tumbling down into a hole or cavity or hollow of some kind. Fortunately for her she was not particularly hurt, just a little bit bruised. Of course she cried out for help and Rufus, the setter, was there at once, barking and calling out at the same time through his transmitter: "Come, its urgent!"

Sylvia, forgetting her fright, found that hilarious. Her companions came running, but were reassured when they saw her smiling face looking up towards them. The prince climbed down immediately, Julian followed him more cautiously. While Adrian was examining Sylvia's bruises and expressing his concern, Julian was looking more closely at what was around them.

It seemed that some old technology was buried there and they had come across it by chance. He found a stick, pushed aside some debris and a weird form appeared, a carriage of some sort. He needed Sophia though to hear her verdict.

"Let's get Sylvia out of here," he said abruptly, "and calm that dog of yours, Rip; it really drives me out of my head!"

After helping Sylvia to get out of the hole and leaving her with Adrian and Rufus, he went back down with Sophia to show her his discovery. They examined it thoroughly.

"It's half buried in the rubble, but I am almost sure that it is a cable car," said Sophia in the end. "They used them to transport people up the mountain slope in the pre-antigrav days. Not for skiers though; skiers used open lifts, had their skies on their feet and jumped once they reached the top. Very exciting; this thing belongs to the museum. I remember now, I found some old maps at the Archives Office the other day, showing the existence of such a line somewhere around here. And Sylvia, fortunately being able to read Cyrillic, on examination of the maps was able to confirm that; it read "cabin lift" in fact."

"Cyrillic?"

"Oh, yes, an old alphabet, nobody uses it nowadays, except language experts and…Sylvia. But in those days people living in this region used exactly that particular script. Anyway, the lift – I can show you some old films from the Archives and you'll get the idea what it looked like at the time. But let's get out of here now, because I'm becoming claustrophobic. And besides, I wish that dog would shut up for a moment!"

She lifted her chin up to observe a shaggy red head bent over the edge of the hole, calling them persistently in a pleading baritone voice.

"Wait a second! What's this?" asked Julian, retrieving a small object, completely caked in mud out of the wreckage.

"I have no idea. We'll look at it later. Let's go now."

"So, what was that all about?" asked Sylvia when they finally climbed out of the hole and Rufus, extremely pleased, had managed to lick the faces of both of them.

"Julian found the remains of the old cabin lift, as you call it."

"Really? That is exciting! I've been on one, not here of course, but in the French Alps!"

"Me too!" exclaimed Adrian, "I used to do a lot of skiing in those years and a lot of hiking."

"So what was it like?" asked Julian.

"The cabin lift? It's actually called a cable car. Basically a number of cabins hanging from a metal rope and being pulled up or down the mountain slope."

"That's one way of putting it," remarked Sophia, trying not very successfully to clear the dust from her clothing, "but I think we should go now. It's been a long day and there is still a lot to do!"

Rufus readily agreed; it was getting rather cold and he did not like to remain in one and the same place for so long.

ENCOUNTERS IN TIME

Over the next couple of days Sophia and Sylvia buried themselves in the archives again and seemed to have been enjoying it immensely. They used to come back with great excitement every time and were keen to tell the others what interesting discoveries they'd made.

"Can you believe," Sylvia was saying, "we found the plans for an amusement park – theme-park, as they were called at the time. It was the first one that was built in this area, a lot later than in the west. And guess what this theme was? Freedom fighters! I remember my grandmother telling me at the time that the country was under foreign rule for centuries and there was always resistance against it; the people kept their language and their religion and eventually they were liberated and a new era started for them. But the theme park takes you back into this dark period of oppression and it's very well thought out! Believe me! I've been to theme parks in my time! It's a pity that they don't exist any more, not as we know them anyway, don't you think, Rip?"

She looked towards Adrian, who was amused by her enthusiasm.

"We've passed that age anyway," he said, "and we have to embrace the future. Enjoy what it has to offer and feel happy that we have this chance."

"We haven't told them about the message yet!" said Sophia, "And that was definitely a very odd thing to happen."

"Oh, maybe an error or something," replied Sylvia, "who knows?"

But Sophia shook her head:

"My dear, errors like that might've been happening in your time, but these days it's very unlikely. I'd find this a very unusual occurrence, if that were indeed an error! Anyway, what surprised me so much was that I got a message from some unknown origin, while I was looking through some old files on some very ancient computer; this could not happen on my communicator, because such messages are automatically deleted, as you all know. The funny thing is that to open it I was supposed to use a password, which it seems consisted of the second part of a formula of some sort. I have it here."

And she produced her E-notepad, on which she had jotted down a few symbols and handed it to Julian. He showed a great interest in the formula:

"That can't be! It's impossible! How on Earth..." he exclaimed looking at the symbols in disbelief, "that's the conclusion to an equation that I've reached after much thought and calculations; it's kept in secret and it's the very basis of my "time-bubble" discovery! We have to open this message immediately and find out who sent it and why!"

He was visibly shaken. Sophia pressed his hand into hers by way of appeasement:

"Julian! Calm down! You can't just run there now! And the only way to open it is to use that same old computer. We can't access it from here! I'll take you there tomorrow first thing in the morning, have patience! I find it even more peculiar now. It seems that someone is trying to get in touch with us, someone who knows exactly where we are and what we are doing!"

"I don't like this at all," replied Julian, "and for the very same reason! We kept the whole business secret; at least I did, for that's absolutely vital!"

He cast a doubtful glance at Adrian.

"Don't look at me, old chap," said Adrian, "I haven't breathed a word to anybody! Not to mention they'd think I were a fool on a wild goose chase, if I admitted to any such thing!"

"What do you mean by that?" Julian asked crossly.

Adrian shifted uneasily in his seat:

"No offence! I don't know a lot about your modern technology, of course, but the whole thing seems to me rather far fetched! And anyway," he rounded on Julian, "who do you think I am, going around and spreading rumours! I've been brought up in a well to do, influential aristocratic family at a time when the press was constantly nosing into our affairs, trying to discover scandals and all that and splash them all over the newspapers! One could not survive in such times, unless one kept one's mouth shut!"

"All right! You've made your point! I suppose we don't have any other option but to wait and see!" Julian said resignedly. "But I don't like it at all."

The computer was very old indeed. Julian had never seen anything so ancient and he was astonished that it was still in working order. Sophia shrugged her shoulders:

"Oh, well, there are always the computer enthusiasts, you know, people who are fascinated by such gadgets and know how to take them apart and, perhaps more importantly, how to put them together again; but I am afraid I am not one of them. I can use them though. It's not that difficult once you are taught how. I knew somebody once, long time ago, who introduced me to ancient technology. Sometimes it comes in handy, you know. Anyway, let's see, I have to connect to the EIN (Earth's Info-Net) and look for my mailbox. That gadget here is called a mouse. You click here and there with it like this..." she briefly demonstrated it to a very impressed Julian who was watching all the proceedings as if they were part of a magician's act, without interrupting her explanations in the mean time:

"Voice commands do not apply. There it is: a message from nowhere or so it seems. You have to type the password in this space, using the keyboard."

"But how? This keyboard as you call it has got some weird signs on it but I am not sure that I know what they are!"

"Use whatever you find appropriate! We have to try and that's the only way!"

"Very well, here goes, I am writing down my formula, but why are there only stars appearing on the screen? It's not working!"

"That's all right, it's a password, that's why it shouldn't be displayed for security reasons. Let's click here now, and…you did it, you did it! It's open now!"

"My dear Sophia and Julian!

This letter comes from the future! Yes, yes, it might be a surprise, but if you are reading these lines, that can only mean one thing: I have succeeded! Mind you, not without your help! But I will not go into details yet; it's a long story. Let's say, that you've always been an inspiration to me, since I was a child. Julian inspired me with his ideas of looking back into the past and Sophia, well, she was above all the decisive factor that made this link possible! I worked hard to establish this communication and am looking forward to hearing from you – that is to say – to get your answer! I shall tell you more later on. Please respond!

Yours from the future
Trajan

"This can't be some sick joke, can it?" asked Sophia.

Julian rubbed his forehead with his fingers:

"No, I don't think so. Too elaborate, and I don't see how it could be done. It has to be true. What do we know? We were arrogantly spying on people from the past and believing that we were great, while somebody else was busy tracing our own path from the future. Ironic, isn't it? But at least some still have their eyes turned back towards the past, I mean would have…how confusing! Somebody out there will be waiting for an answer. We should drop them a few lines at least and see what happens. We should ask some questions too. I have a lot of questions."

"But it's so incredible!" exclaimed Sophia, "I always thought that I had an open mind, but this! When I think about it, Julian, your coming into my life started this whole chain of unbelievable events. Could I have possibly foreseen this when I met you that afternoon by the sea? I think not. But are we going to tell Adrian and Sylvie? Could we trust them to keep it secret with the Adapt Centre always nosing around?"

"We have to tell them. They are part of it all now. Don't you see?" Julian looked at her impatiently, "I guess this Trajan knows everything about them anyway. And we are the bridge in the middle of it – we are the present, linking the future and the past. It all makes sense to me."

Some time later they were all four sitting in the hotel bar, having a drink after the evening meal. The sound of jazz had a calming effect on everyone. Nobody spoke for a while.

"The whole thing is now entering the realm of science-fiction," said Adrian at length.

"But it's so thrilling! More so than in my wildest dreams!" exclaimed Sylvia.

"Do you actually realise what this will mean?" replied Julian, "The end of life in the way that we know it! The beginning of a new era!"

Little did they understand his words at the time. Sylvia was bursting with questions she wanted to ask. They were debating the consequences of knowing too much about the future – was it going to change anything? The eternal question, since transportation in time was first considered. Nobody had ever given a definitive answer. Nor was it likely ever to be answered.

"At least we were only looking into the past," said Sophia, referring to Julian's experiment.

"So far that's true, but there are ways to change that and look towards the future," explained Julian, "and nobody knows what would happen in that case. In the hands of the wrong person such knowledge becomes very dangerous indeed!"

"It would be a pity if you were to destroy what you've created after so much effort," remarked Adrian.

"It's not a question to destroy, but perhaps to keep it secret and only reveal it to members of the family – say from father to son, if I ever have a son," he sighed.

"I wonder if we would ever get another message from our future friend," Sophia wondered.

The second letter arrived promptly the next day:

Hello again!

This is scheduled to reach you on the following day, to give you some time to get used to the thought, so to speak. And I have some more news for you – very interesting too! It seems that we live in exciting times, or more likely everything comes together now. I also had a communication from the future! I was actually able to speak with a real person who got in touch with me at the same time that I was establishing a link with you! It's not surprising of course, for this is a historic moment, the concept of time has changed, life itself has changed! Let's see what this new life has in store for all of us!

Greetings from the future
Trajan

"We should concentrate now on the experiment," said Julian, "these other developments have to wait; we have just a couple more days left to prepare."

"But we are so excited," exclaimed Sylvia, "we want to know more about the future!"

"And what about the past then? Don't you want to find out more about that? About your grandmother?"

"Gran! Of course I want to discover more! I am…was very fond of her."

"Well then! Let's plan things! Have you found out something about the place in question, Sophia?"

"It's difficult. It's not even possible to rent a space there. This area that you indicated was part of a public garden in the past. Now it has been developed."

"Developed? How do you mean?" asked Julian perplexed.

"Developed, i.e. it has been built over. It would've been fine if we could have rented a flat there or something, but the owner actually wants to sell, not to rent…"

"That has been taken care of," said Adrian suddenly," I am buying it."

"What?" exclaimed Sophia and Julian.

"Why not? It's a nice location and I reckon it's a sound investment. We can rent it out afterwards if we like and use it when we come here again."

"Here is a man who doesn't waste his time," remarked Julian, "why not indeed?"

He looked at Sophia.

"Yes, I did my bit!" she said. "There was actually a cafeteria there in the past."

"In the public garden?" asked Julian.

"In the public garden; it was an open air cafeteria in fact – very much 'the in thing' at the time. It was precisely there that Phillip proposed."

"Really? A marriage proposal in a cafeteria! That's not very romantic!"

"Probably not. But it seems that it was connected with some sentimental memories."

"Fair enough! Let's go for it then. When can I move my stuff there? Have you thought about that, Adrian?"

"As a matter of fact I did! I signed the contract this morning and we can move in tomorrow or even now if you particularly want to."
"Great! Tomorrow will be fine!"

They were all sitting at a round table almost like the knights from the famous legend, Sylvia thought, or rather like participants in a séance, summoning up the spirits of loved ones. And the headgear also looked ridiculous; Adrian especially resembled some sort of surreal Don Quixote with his lean aristocratic face, featuring deep set eyes and Roman nose, framed by that bizarre helmet. She made an effort to keep a straight face more out of fear that Julian would exclude her from the experiment than for any other reason. Julian was not looking at her though, too busy to get everything ready. He bent over, adjusting some dials, when without any warning, it all started to happen.

For both Sylvia and Adrian it was the first time they had experienced it and they found it almost unbearable to be suddenly thrown like that into an unfathomable whirlpool where right or left, up or down, light or dark and even time, were rendered absolutely meaningless; they couldn't feel their bodies anymore and only their minds were being hurled about till eventually they popped out not unlike corks from champagne bottles, into a strange world hundreds of years earlier. Julian and Sophia had already been through this experience but were still relieved to be free of it. They all felt as if they were floating aimlessly about and it was only Julian's calm voice that gave everybody a focal point. Curiosity was also taking over and they looked about at their surroundings.

There they were in a little cafeteria similar to those they've seen in old films, though for Adrian and Sylvia it was more like what they were used to: small tables – some inside, others, mostly taken - outside, simple chairs, plain porcelain cups and saucers. It was a rather crowded place with windows facing a huge ancient building. Sophia and Sylvia knew it to be the Palais of Culture. There was a vast open space around it – terraces and gardens, and yet it was very busy.

Some event was going on; it seemed to be an improvised open-air concert. The crowds were absolutely ecstatic, everybody was singing, waving blue flags and shouting slogans in a long forgotten language. It was almost like watching a very old news footage, almost but not exactly. Our "time-travellers" without the physical constraint of their bodies, had the feeling that they were really becoming one with the crowds, at least emotionally if not physically, such was the spell, cast by that music.

Sophia spotted them first:
"Look! There they are," she cried, "she is wearing a pale blue dress and he…"
But the others had already seen them.
"You've got the time wrong," said Sylvia, "but that's better! For this is actually when they first met! It all comes back to me. Gran told me they first bumped into each other at this "meeting" – that's what they called this demonstration; he chatted her up and invited her for a cup of coffee and the rest is history!"
"A meeting!" exclaimed Sophia, "but of course, a meeting it is. I do know that time period! There were great changes at the time, a political dictatorship had just been replaced by a more democratic system; it happened all around the Eastern region at the same time. "
"I wouldn't call it exactly democratic, this new system," remarked Adrian.

But Sophia didn't have time to reply, because the couple were approaching them and suddenly they felt they had bodies again, but not their own! Sylvia and Sophia suddenly saw the world through the eyes of Zara and Julian and Adrian – through Philip's eyes. The next few moments they tried to adjust themselves to their new perspectives. Then to understand what was being said, because the conversation had been continuing unhindered by their invasion, and strange as it might seem, they were just witnessing it, not taking any part in it.

Zara and Philip were conversing in English – a language which was now incorporated into the Universal and which Sylvia and Adrian spoke fluently (in fact Sylvia was brought up with this language), Sophia had quite a good understanding of it and Julian had a fairly good idea of what was being discussed.

"It seems that they are singing that song again," Philip was saying, "sounds nice but I have not the slightest idea what it is all about?"

"It starts with the line: "45 years that's enough! The time belongs to us!" and that says it all really. We are not going to put up with the old regime any more, we want change!"

Zara's eyes were sparkling. She led her companion to a table that was just becoming available and ordered some coffee and fruit juice.

"People believed in those changes at the time. But later there came disillusionment", remarked Sophia, "more rights maybe, but also greater insecurity…"

"I am very optimistic about the future of your country, it seems that young people especially know what they want and change is certainly needed," said Philip," I didn't expect to find this here, I have to admit, but rather, stagnation, lack of initiative, indifference…It's all been a real eye-opener!"

"I am pleased to hear you say this. I am proud of my country and I honestly believe that our place is with the West. But I also realise that we've always been somewhat underestimated…"

"Trouble is, that we, the westerners, don't know enough about Eastern Europe," replied Philip ruefully, "we don't see a lot about it in the news, in fact next to nothing. This is the first East European country that I've ever visited. And that's only because there is this biannual event, the one I was telling you about – The International Biannual Forum of Architects, which takes place here, in Sofia. It's been great! I met all these people from all over the world, including a well-known Russian architect, with whom I had a very interesting discussion; fortunately he spoke English, because I don't know a word in his language! Anyway, I am very happy with my visit here, and I would like to come again very soon; maybe have a touring holiday or something? They've been telling me about some fascinating places around here...What would you suggest?"

"You should go to the Rila monastery, if you haven't seen it yet."

"Oh, yes, that was one of the sights recommended; I saw some pictures in fact, very impressive!"

"It's even more so to see it for real. It's not that far from Sofia – couple of hours probably. Have you got a car at your disposal?"

"Unfortunately not. Besides I have no idea whereabouts that place is and what is probably worse don't speak a word of your language...unless I could find a guide who can take me there..."

"Oh!" exclaimed Adrian suddenly, "he is making his move at last! And she is going to go for it!"

Zara looked at Philip and after a minute or two of hesitation proposed to drive him herself.

"I have only a small Trabant, though, and I don't think you will like it."

"What is a Trabant?" asked Julian.

"A small East European car, German in fact, very simple, very basic," replied Adrian. "Everybody was making jokes about them, even their owners; but they were cheap to run and did the job...great car the old Trabi, became as much of an icon as the Mini or the Beatle."

He sighed, his thoughts lapsing down memory lane.

"I always wanted to try a Trabant," Philip was saying in the meantime.

"That's your opportunity then!"

Suddenly everything disappeared and Adrian and Sylvia, Julian and Sophia were plunged once again into the tunnel-whirlpool and afterwards back into their own time. As Sylvia remarked some moments later: "Peeping Tom has had his fun and was chased away; dating is a private business and Zara and Philip should be left alone to get on with it."

WHO ARE WE TO CHANGE THE FUTURE

Sophia was sitting behind her desk, staring at the wall, but no inspiration was coming. The wall, like the other ones in her study was displaying the 3D image of a landscape, this time it was from mount Vitosha, which had just replaced the view of the sandy beach, favoured last week. She had lots of work to do, but her thoughts were back in Sofia and she was still pondering over the events that had happened there.

She laid her fingers on the smooth surface of her desk and it came to life. It was a screen now, waiting for her command to display any information that she might want.

"Jeeves (that was how she addressed her computer), show me the family archives; Philip Fitzwilliam, biography. Arrange the major events of his life in a column to the left; now display the biography of Zara Mihailovska-Fitzwilliam, following the same pattern to the right. That's it."

Sophia looked thoughtfully at the screen.

"Zara and Philips married life was a success story," she considered, "but what about their descendants? Some of them achieved fame, some were failures. Genetic structure, family background might be important prerequisites, but not the be all and end all of everything. Each individual has to struggle throughout their life to discover themselves, the way a new territory is discovered, and without this ultimate knowledge, happiness is unattainable."

"Jeeves! Display now the family tree, starting from them and finishing with the last of their descendants…,"Sophia ordered.

She knew her family tree by heart. But looking at it gave her a sense of permanence, a firm standpoint in this ever-changing world.

"I exist here and now," she said, "I am willing to look back into the past with equanimity for I can't change a thing. But the future is a different matter. A window into the future! It sounds great, but is it wise even to have as much as a glimpse of it?"

The door opened to let Sylvia in. Sophia smiled; for once, Sylvia had chosen her moment well. There could be no interruption so welcome and the high spirited girl – the most preferred interloper.

"Well?"

"I've just come to see how you are doing. You've been hidden away for ages; no lunch, no sign of life. Julian doesn't dare to disturb you, but I thought I'd better check up on you. You don't mind me doing that, do you? I come from a different century; different customs, different lifestyle, everything is different there."

"Yes, the past *is* a different country, my dear. And yes, I am OK, just mulling things over, that's all."

Sylvia looked at the screen in awe:

"Wow, that's a photo of Granddad, when he was young! And three dimensional too! Cool! Where did you get it from?"

"Oh, the wonders of modern technology! These days it's quite easy to have an old photo transformed into a 3D image. So you remember your Granddad?"

"Of course! But when he was a lot older, grey and weathered…He taught me to play badminton. We used to play out on the lawn there," Sylvia said, pointing towards the garden outside, "but it was warmer then. He taught me to swim too. We had an open air swimming pool back then; it was much nicer than the one you've got now."

She sighed wistfully and resumed after a pause:

"Kids at school were envious, calling me a rich bitch and the like. But I suppose, we *were* rich. Granddad had won some competition or another for a fancy public building he designed. That earned him heaps of money. He bought this land from a millionaire whose wife didn't quite like it here and wanted to move to Florida."

Sophia was standing motionless, all ears, not daring to interrupt this fascinating narrative of Sylvia's.

"Gran was always joking about it: "a land scorned by millionaires," she used to say, "but with the seal of approval from the Fitzwilliams". Granddad built the house on the site and Gran designed the interiors. It took some time apparently. It's a big house! Dad used to say that in his earliest childhood memories it was still a bit of a building site. But look at it now! Still standing after all these years! Granddad would've been really proud if he was still alive to see it."

"Oh, I am sure he would've loved it! Despite the changes, I believe each consecutive owner has been extremely careful to preserve the original concept of this Mediterranean villa. I've lived here all my life and find it the perfect retreat from all the hustle and bustle. But anyway! Let's go and have a bite to eat, because I am starving! As you rightly observed I missed my lunch."

They headed to another part of the house, where the kitchen was. Julian was there, pouring himself a drink:

"Oh, I see, Sylvia managed to persuade you to emerge from your den!"

"Don't be flippant, Julian! I needed some time on my own. It dawned on me that we are in a precarious position. I still don't know what we are supposed to do. As you have justly pointed out, this knowledge we have, is extremely dangerous. Whichever way you look at it, knowing the future is going to affect one's actions and we haven't got a clue what the consequences may be. This is not a trifling matter."

"My dear Sophie, you take these things far too seriously! The guys from the future know what they are talking about. They see it as an exciting development! There isn't any problem really. It's just a new phase in our lives. You shouldn't be so fearful of change!"

"But the consequences, Julian, think about the consequences...," Sophia reminded him, while buttering her bread with quick, precise movements of her hand; her sandwiches usually looked more like artistic creations than mere culinary products.

Julian looked at the glass he was holding as if wondering about having another drink:

"What consequences? Far ahead of us, there in the future, whatever happens here and now, has already had whatever impact it was going to have there and then. We can't change a damn thing, like it or not. For them it has all happened already, for us it's not even been written yet!"

"It's so complicated! I don't understand it at all!"

"What is there to understand?" asked Julian impatiently, "as far as they are concerned, we have already affected their lives; for them there isn't any other reality. Having their glimpses of the past, they might find out for example what you had/will have for breakfast a couple of years from now and so what of it? You haven't even decided on your breakfast tomorrow morning, let alone 2 years in the future. They might even share this information with you. So what? You might decide to be contrary and instead of toast and jam, have a croissant. So far so good, you say, I changed the future."

He drummed on the counter with his fingers:

"You haven't changed a bloody thing. You can't even be sure that the info you've gotten from them in the first instance, was correct. They might have been mistaken or else they might have interests at odds with yours and they might lead you astray for some purpose you don't know anything about."

He paced back and forth, pursuing his train of thought:

"You wouldn't know any better even if you had a crystal ball and could actually look into it. To steal a look into

79

somebody else's life is not the same as to experience it first hand. You are not as omnipotent as a god to manage such a feat.

Whatever you think, I don't believe you can change the future even if you know beforehand what's going to happen. It's not possible. Just as you can't change the past either. Don't shake your head like that, come on, you are the historian, you should know better.

Revolutionary changes occur all the time in human history. Humankind gets shaken up a bit every now and then, but every cloud has a silver lining, life goes on, we adapt and we carry on regardless.

Let's take the Internet for example. In the 20th century its launch was exactly one of those happenings that had such great repercussions on everyone's life. All of a sudden people had all this information at their disposal and were able to conduct business online and all the rest of it. The so called globalization was facilitated. Our life today would be unthinkable without the discovery of the Internet and its unlimited possibilities."

"But the Net is different from looking into the future!"

"But is it that different? We are dealing with information here. To know what's happening on the other side of the world or to know what's happening in your own future? It's all information and you act accordingly based on that information. Every decision you make in your life depends on the available data, no matter what its source may be.

The better informed you are, the better the option you'll choose. But beware! As always if you are flooded with too much data, you may become so overwhelmed that things get out of control; as was the case with my last laboratory experiment when I tried to take every possible variable into account instead of working only with the most important parameters that were crucial to it. Well, what I am trying to say is this: don't complicate, keep it simple."

"Cool!" Sylvia started clapping her hands in applause and Sophia joined in:

"Wow, all this coming from you, my technological wizard? You *are* full of surprises, or should I say deep philosophical ideas? But I have to admit, it sounds almost convincing."

Julian pretended to be offended:

"Only "almost"? So I've wasted all this time thinking out the best arguments in support of my theory! All in vain! Won't you offer me a sandwich at least?"

"As a consolation prize? Certainly!"

Sophia was laughing aloud when she started on the second sandwich. She felt relieved as she always did after such a repartee with Julian. Sylvia left them to it and went in search of her robot.

Julian stood beside Sophia and stroked her cheek.

"You can always talk to me when you feel like this, instead of fending me off," he said quietly.

She smiled, but did not reply. Life had made her wary of giving away too many confidences, of too much shared soul searching. Only recently she had gotten over a very deep depression. Julian had been instrumental in this healing process, by involving her in his experiments, and he knew it only too well. However he shouldn't push her too hard yet. It had been in any case a wonder that he had any success at all, where others had failed.

Sophia remembered how she had been quite suspicious at the time: she had thought of it as being some elaborate plot put together by her therapist to get her on the mend. She smiled again, putting the final touches to her sandwich and handing it to Julian:

"Believe it or not, but once I suspected you of being somehow in league with my therapist. You came up with those fantastic stories about time-bubbles and such and I didn't know what to make of it and, and…"

"And you thought it would be better to take it all with a pinch of salt," said Julian biting with relish into the

81

sandwich, "I liked you the more for it. You are a reasonable, no nonsense woman and certainly not one to allow herself to be taken for a ride. Even by someone like me."

He looked so comical munching happily and nodding his head that Sophia couldn't help it and started to laugh again.
Later when he had finished his snack, Julian rinsed his fingers and announced with a grin:
"Now, haven't we forgotten something?"
"What do you mean?"
"In all our excitement with messages from the future and glimpses of the past, there was one tiny little thing you completely forgot about."
"What's that?"
"That little something we found on the mountain."
"Ah! On our trip to Sofia! In the cabin lift! And what did you decide that was?"
"I decided that we had a very big stroke of luck. What I found there was a very old little gadget, a real antique in fact. It contains data in the form of photos and text. I had to find an old computer to be able to view it, but that's all done now and we can go and have a look at it, if you are in the mood."

There was a huge quantity of photos, stored on the little device. Soon they realized that it would take a lot of time to view them all. Most of them showed various objects, mostly coins, but also silver plates, tankards, even weapons.
"It looks like a museum collection," said Sophia, "but here is a man's face too. What does he have to do with all these artifacts? I wonder…For some reason or another, I don't think he is a very nice person that one."
"There is a document here. What do you make of it?" asked Julian.
Sophia examined it carefully:

"It looks like a list of some sort, but it makes no sense to me. Those are dates, but the rest...Wait! It might be a code. Let's apply my code breaker. Copy this page and we'll see."

The code breaker didn't disappoint them. Soon they had a list of names to go with the dates. Sophia fed all the data into her history data bank and they waited a couple of minutes for the result. Eventually they had it.

"A criminal gang!" exclaimed Julian. "Now it makes perfect sense. So what they have done is smuggled these precious artifacts out of the country to sell them to antique dealers abroad. It seems to have been a huge operation, bearing in mind the quantity of these objects. Why did they have to do it?"

"For money, of course. People will do anything for money. I agree, it's such a pity that treasures like these are not all kept in museums, where they belong, but get locked away in private collections just to satisfy the vanity of rich people. Sometimes somebody's guilty conscience or the generosity of an inheritor enables us to see and admire these riches, but in most cases, they remain hidden away or quickly change owners when cash is needed."

"I still can't understand why this data storage device was left on the mountain where we found it?" Julian wondered.

"It must've been lost there. But let's see! Ah! Look at this!"

A short documentary was describing the events prior to the arrest of the nucleus of this notorious criminal ring. A young police officer working under cover had been following one of the main suspects. He had tracked him up the mountain amidst a group of skiers and then trailed him down the ski slope.

Nobody ever found out what exactly had happened there between the two men. The bodies were found a lot later after an extensive search.

Julian said pensively:

"He must've dropped the storage device in the scuffle. To be found by us centuries later. What a waste! Both of them young, everything going for them. Especially the cop. Look at him! He's just a boy."

It was later that evening and Julian was sitting by himself in the library, his favorite haunt. Sophia had gone to bed and Sylvia had just followed her. Adrian, who had been out for a breath of air with his dog Rufus, came in. He strolled towards the drinks cabinet and poured himself some port:
"Fancy one?"
"I'd rather have some whisky," replied Julian.
"Ice?"
"No, just the way it comes."
"So! Sophie is in one of her moods again, I take it?"
This coming from Adrian sounded like a question, but was in fact meant more like a statement.
"She'll be alright; I am not worried about her."
"What's eating you then, old chap?"
"I was thinking about that smugglers story, we uncovered. Remember, we talked about it at dinner and you even said that you knew the case."
"Oh, yes," replied Adrian, "it was in all the newspapers at the time and was making the headlines for a week or so till some other sensational news replaced it - to my brother's relief."
Julian sat upright:
"Your brother? Why? What did he have to do with it?"
"Oh, he knew one of the dealers, implicated in that business. You know, he was an antique collector, had an extensive collection which eventually got handed down to me. I mean after my grand nephew passed away at the ripe old age of 95. Don't tell me you didn't know that! I am sure I must've mentioned it…at least in passing."

"Adrian, please! Can we start from the beginning? You were saying that your brother was involved with that dealer of stolen/smuggled goods…"

"It wasn't as bad as it sounds, old chap, but yes, on the whole he was a bit unscrupulous, my brother was. Of course he didn't know where all those objects were coming from, "no questions asked" et cetera; you know how it was in those times…"

"Frankly, no, I don't know, but I am getting the picture. Carry on!"

"He'd bought a couple of silver platters from him and afterwards there was a big racket about giving them back. I can't remember what happened. I was sick at the time, you understand, dying in fact, so it wasn't exactly my top priority and I didn't take any particular interest in the matter."

"And?"

"And you know the rest. I ended up in the Deep Freeze and next thing I knew, I was out of it a couple of centuries or so later, but hooray, I was cured, I met a nice young girl and I am about to marry her."

"Yes, but what about that inheritance, you mentioned?"

"Julian, I didn't think you were so mercenary! Are you saying that you are not going to give the bride away, unless I have a couple of millions on the side! I told you already, when I came out of the Deep Freeze, there was only a grand nephew of mine alive, but he died conveniently, shortly afterwards and I finally inherited the estate."

"Adrian, don't be an ass! What about those platters? Are they still in that collection?"

"Do you know, I haven't got the slightest idea! But I can find out!"

"You do that! Because I have some pictures here of platters and coins and a whole big hoard of treasures smuggled out of their country of origin and sold to rich bastards!"

"Calm down, man! I wasn't awfully fond of my brother, but still! Stop calling him names, please! If we find those platters, what do you want me to do with them?"

"Take them back to where they belong of course! The museum of antiquity in Sofia would love to have them, I'm sure!"

A month later Sophia was standing in front of her screen again but this time with a smile on her face. Adrian joined her.

"Look, Adrian, there they are! I can now go for a virtual tour of the museum and see them from the comfort of my home, or go there in person and see them for myself; after all, there is nothing quite like the real thing! Are you not pleased? After all these years, hidden in a bank vault, where nobody could enjoy them, not even their owner, they are out now, on display to be seen and admired!"

"Yes, I am pleased. Of course I am. You can afford to be charitable when you are rich. For those poor devils dishonest or not, it was a question of earning a living; just these platters alone would've made them a fortune; but instead they ended up in prison or dead.

And before you start making any plans for the rest of my collection, I have some news for you. I am already making arrangements to open a museum myself and to put it on display there and you can come and see it in person or go for a virtual tour from the comfort of your own home and so could anybody else who is interested in it. And, for that matter, no, don't say a word to dissuade me or try to tell me that you have found out that there is some other party that might or might not have a prior claim to any of my exhibits. I don't want to know."

"My dear Adrian, I just wanted to say that I heartily approve of your idea. In fact Sylvia told me already. I am pleased for her too, for you have promised to involve her in the design and arrangement of the place. She is very good at that sort of thing and will enjoy it."

Adrian took her hand and lifted it with exaggerated gallantry to his lips:

"I should've known that she'd tell you everything and spoil the surprise, but never mind. I have made such an effort to please you, my dear lady. It's a relief to hear that I have succeeded. And don't you worry about the future. It's in the making – here and now, and we'll do what to our knowledge is for the best, the way we've always done so in the past."

THE HIDDEN TREASURE

It was a nice autumnal day, but Sophia had had a restless night and wasn't in the best of moods. Julian and Sylvia went out for a walk, taking Adrian's dog Rufus with them. Sophia decided to do some work, but an hour later she was still fiddling with her wall size screens, changing the landscapes and not finding one that she wanted.

She had screens on each and every wall of her study, as that was the current fashion and an impressive space panorama was usually her choice, but that day nothing seemed to please her. Eventually one of the screens started to flicker – and the "There is a malfunction"-sign appeared on it. That irritated Sophia even more, she switched the thing off, then on again, but it still wouldn't work.

At one point – she wasn't sure what she did exactly – the screen simply slid aside and all of a sudden she had just an empty wall in front of her. And empty walls were not what you would see in your everyday life if you lived in that century. In fact in that time walls were not built with bricks and mortar any more. New and more effective materials were used and screens were incorporated into them. But living in such an old building made it necessary for some adjustments to be made in order to bring it up to date.

Sophia was sentimentally attached to "Elounda", the house that had been built by one of her ancestors and family home for quite a few generations. Each of her predecessors had made some improvements so as to be in sync with the times, but no major structural changes were ever attempted. So the screens had been added in later times. Following customary practice any of them could be used either for communication, or as a computer monitor/ home cinema screen and when out of active use would display whatever image was chosen – moving or still.

It seemed that now something was seriously wrong with her screen for it to do what it did. Sophia stared at the wall in front of her. She remembered that in times past people decorated their walls or hung pictures on them. The surface was actually quite rough to the touch when she moved her fingers along it.

"What on earth..." she started to say, when she realised that there was an almost invisible gap in this wall, forming a sort of frame. This must be indicating a door, she thought. It was old though, very old and she wasn't sure how to open it. She thought she'd better call Julian.

"A door in the wall?" asked Julian.

"A door in the wall!" exclaimed Sylvia, "so it is still there!"

"What are you talking about?"

But Sylvia was running back towards the house. Julian and Sophia followed her. They entered the study exactly in time to see the door in question opening or rather turning on its axis to expose a neatly stacked bookcase on the other side. They were speechless for a moment or two.

"But that's unbelievable! What a treasure!" exclaimed Sophia.

"You can say that," Sylvia was obviously proud of herself, "I am glad that you've kept it."

"These books here would really cost a fortune nowadays," said Julian, "that's not an exaggeration, but how did you know about them?"

"It's simple," replied Sylvia, giving them a sly look, "they are there, because of me," and then she added, seeing their astonishment, "what I mean is that they were hidden from me, but not very successfully as you can see."

"Tell us everything at once!" said Julian.

"All right, but can I have a snack first? I am starving!"

She burst out laughing seeing the effect of her request on her audience:

"No? All right, all right, I'll tell you now, here it goes. I learned to read when I was 5 or 6 and there was no stopping me, once I got started. They were very proud of me, the adults, and they just let me get on with it. I was reading everything and anything I could put my hands on. Then one nice day, I was 10 at the time, my daddy discovered that I was reading "La Reine Margot"- that's "Queen Margot" by Dumas," she added, observing both faces glaze over with incomprehension. She was going to enjoy this.

"I still can't understand," she pursued, "why he was so annoyed: "Somebody should supervise this child's reading, this is not at all appropriate for her age" et cetera; that kind of crap. Anyway, my Gran tried to defend me, said she used to read books like that when she was my age with no ill effect whatsoever, but no, my father would have none of it: "Times have changed, mother. Besides I am the parent now, therefore responsible for Sylvia's upbringing; I am to decide what's best for her."

Sylvia did the impersonation of her father so well, that Julian tried in vain to suppress his laughter. He had been shown some old footage of a public speech once made by Sylvia's father and thought the latter was a rather pompous git; Sylvia's narrative confirmed his opinion, which he however refrained from sharing with the others.

"So they built this "cache" and thought I'd never find it," Sylvia was saying, "but little did they know me. Once I located it, I read everything here. Inevitably my Gran found out eventually. But she knew how to keep a secret. So now you know."

"So what's the big deal about this "Margot" book and the rest of them?" asked Julian, "Pornography?"

"Oh, Good heavens, no! Not at all! What an idea! Just romantic novels! Exciting stuff! I take it you haven't read it then? No? I envy you! You'll have the time of your life! Look! There's "La Reine Margot", the English version and here is "Le Comte de Monte Cristo", that is "The Count of

Monte Cristo" also in English, both written by the same author, Dumas, but he was actually a Frenchman; there are a few more novels by him and look here, this is one by Daphne du Maurier, and she wasn't French at all, notwithstanding the name; but Maupassant here – he was definitely French and, oh boy, wasn't he naughty! But this one is in French, so I wonder why it is here? The French stuff was not hidden from me, you see, because at the time my French was not up to much and…but where are you guys?"

But Julian and Sophia were gone. They thought it better to leave her with her newly found treasure. Besides Sophia wanted to check up on these books on the Net and Julian was wondering if there were appropriate versions in Universal, he wouldn't be able to cope very well with the old English…

Sophia found Julian and Adrian later that day drinking coffee in the conservatory, with Rufus keeping them company, his head on his master's knee.

"So what's the news?" asked Julian. "Adrian here is saying there is not a great deal for any parent to get so excited about over those books of Sylvia; popular novels at the time, they're a good read, so what's the point of hiding them from the kid?"

Sophia shrugged her shoulders:

"True, true, you could say that, but you don't know the moral principles of our family, pretty strait-laced all of them, strict and over the top, especially where the children were concerned. I was also brought up in this fashion. Not that it mattered a lot. Funny, when Sylvia was telling us her story I thought of myself at her age and the antics I got up to. Watching all the virtual reality films, which my father considered unsuitable for my age, no matter that most of my friends had already seen them."

"And what about this Margot?"

"Apparently Margot did live in some distant period of the past, I'm not going to bore you with the finer details. She was a beauty and a Royal into the bargain, a real Queen in fact, reputed to have had numerous affaires. The one described in the book is the most famous of them all, because her lover paid with his life for the privilege. Some of her other lovers allegedly also met similar fates, for it is said that she kept their hearts embalmed in special little boxes...Very romantic stuff, I tell you, and if anything I would encourage young girls to read it, because most romantic notions seem to have almost disappeared these days."

"But, Sophia, this stuff was already quite passé in our time!" exclaimed Adrian, "by at least a century or more. I mean, the time when the books were written. They probably belonged more to Sylvia's great-grandmother or something. The current trend coming out in my time, was actually quite nasty, and some of it definitely not suitable for impressionable young girls."

"Perhaps her father was the old fashioned type and over-protective. Does it matter? The point I want to make is that those books are indeed very rare and I have to insure them accordingly. We rely on you, Adrian to keep this matter secret, it is important!"

"What, Dumas's books are rare these days you say? That's unbelievable! Granted he was given a place in the Panthéon, but still...who would've thought it?"

"The Panthéon?"

"Yes, Julian, the Panthéon, that neoclassical church in the Latin Quarter of Paris, that functions as a burial place for the famous sons of France. As far as I know it's still there?"

"Ah, that Panthéon! I see. Oh yes, it's still there of course, but I don't think that they bury anybody there anymore. As for this Dumas having being buried there, well, what can I say? Unfortunately I have never had the chance to read any of his books, so I don't know if he deserves this honour or not."

"Adrian," Sophia said impatiently, "any printed materials these days are rare and very valuable. They are not produced any more, you know."

"Oh dear! In what society did I end up? No books? No printed materials! How incredible! I just had not realised till now that you don't make books any more. What do you read in your spare time then?"

"We do read books, Adrian! But they don't produce them in this format. Paper is very expensive. Do you know how many trees had to be chopped down to produce those books? Anyway, you've seen the books we've got now. You've read some of them."

"What, this electronic crap? No, really! I can read them, but not for more than half an hour at a time. It gives me headaches. I've been asking for print-outs of various sorts and wondered why people were giving me funny looks and saying they were not available."

"Reading books these days shouldn't cause you any headache; maybe in the past, when technology was not so advanced, but now? Unlikely! The screens have evolved so much since your time; you admitted yourself that they are not at all like those you remember," Sophia countered him.

"Perhaps you guys are used to them. I am not. It takes me a lot longer to read stuff from the screen than if it were printed on ordinary paper. Besides it's just not the same. I mean what pleasure is there in gazing at a screen trying to concentrate on a text? It's not like watching a film or playing a computer game. There is something special about holding the printed book, touching each page when turning it, inhaling that scent, especially strong in an old book…"

"How bizarre!" said Julian, "You find the smell of decaying paper pleasant? No, not for me, thanks."

"It sounds almost poetic," remarked Sophia, "I haven't thought about it in that way, but you have a point there, I suppose. For somebody like me, who occasionally deals with old books and artefacts in general, they seem special indeed."

"But, Adrian, if you find reading from a screen difficult, you can always ask to have it read to you or ask for an enactment. Haven't they explained this to you at the Adapt Centre?" asked Julian.

"Come to think about it, they did mention something about enactments, but I have to admit I wasn't at all sure what they were talking about."

"You just have to ask the computer. There are all sorts of options. You can even participate in your favourite plays."

"Really? Now, that is amazing – to be able to fulfil my childhood dreams for a career on the stage! Who would've believed it? Although on second thoughts, I better not. It's hardly going to be that different from the virtual computer worlds we had in my time. I was quite hooked at one stage; rather disturbing if you think about it; spending most of my time dwelling in some artificial computer reality, conducting business, having lots of friends that I'd never met in person and even a girlfriend. Real escapism that was, believe you me."

At that moment Sylvia burst into the room. She was very excited:

"Look what I've found!"

Three faces and a silky red muzzle turned towards her and looked astonished at the box she held in her white hands. It was made of wood and looked like a real antique.

"Well?" said Adrian finally, "It's a box."

"Yes, but not any old box. This is a treasure chest!"

Sylvia opened it triumphantly and displayed the contents.

"Old jewellery," said Julian, "rather old fashioned too; belongs to a museum."

Sylvia wasn't impressed:

"Tell him, Sophie!"

"I am afraid he is right, my dear."

"But why?" asked Adrian, "These are precious stones," he was looking at a diamond necklace, "this would've cost a fortune in my time."

"Not any more," replied Sophia, "precious stones lost their value a long time ago. We have other substitutes these days."

"They are precious to me," Sylvia objected, "Gran promised to leave them to me. As it was…"

"Well, you keep them then," Sophia said quickly.

"You don't mind?"

"Of course not. You found them after all. Besides, a promise is a promise. But let's see what else is there at the bottom of this box."

"The box itself is quite interesting," remarked Julian.

"Of course, it is. Look at the craftsmanship! Don't tell me you don't value such objects these days!" exclaimed Adrian.

"Old artefacts are always valued," replied Sophia, "but I am not an expert. And it all depends on the collectors market of the moment. How rare the object is for example."

Adrian lifted the box up and examined it carefully. He caressed the wood reverently and tapped the bottom with his finger:

"Secret compartment as well, brilliant!"

"You are impossible!" exclaimed Sylvia, slapping his hand playfully, "I kept this bit for the end!"

"We'll leave it for the end then, don't fret," said Adrian, "but let's concentrate on the exterior for now and try to guess what it is made of. Let me think and don't tell me!" he waved a hand towards Sylvia who was just about to say something.

"I think this comes from Morocco and if I am not mistaken it's made from the root of thuya!" he announced triumphantly.

Sophia and Julian looked at Sylvia for confirmation. She had intended to impress them with her knowledge, but now Adrian had stolen her thunder.

"Right as always," the girl admitted begrudgingly, "but let me show you the double bottom now."

But Adrian raised his hand:

"Wait, wait! Young people today, so impetuous! We haven't finished yet. Note: silver incrustation, floral motifs, mother of pearl decoration, top quality. I'll tell you this, Sophie, your ancestors had an eye for a good investment. The Moroccans produced a lot of thuya goods for the mass market; in fact this type of wood is unique to Morocco and they developed a very profitable industry out of it."

"But if it was mass produced, it's not going to be very valuable, is it?" remarked Julian, who was following the conversation with interest, "my father has a collection of old wooden objects, but I think they are worthless."

"It depends on all sorts of things, old man - the demand, condition, rarity, and of course quality! This box here is quite rare, possibly custom made."

"Don't look at me," said Sylvia, pleased to be the centre of attention again, "I don't know is the answer. It was my Gran's and she prized it highly as far as I can remember, but whether it was just for sentimental reasons or because it was valuable, I have no idea."

"Look!" Sophia exclaimed, "there is an old manuscript on the bottom. Don't touch it. It's fragile. I'll get my gloves out."

"There is decaying paper for you, my friend! I still don't find it particularly appealing," Julian was saying to Adrian, "do you?"

"It's old!" Adrian replied excitedly, "Look at the date! I was alive at that time! Would you believe it?"

Sylvia in the meantime was scrutinizing the paper now spread in front of them: ·

"It's Gran's handwriting. It must be one of her short stories. She used to write them on odd bits of paper, anything really that she had close to hand, because, she used to say, when you have an inspiration, you must seize the moment, don't let it pass you by.   She must've shoved it in the box afterwards and forgotten all about it. She was like that."

HALLOWEEN

The Earth looked lovely. Gleaming like a jewel on dark velvet, he thought, exactly as the old metaphor went. They admired it silently for awhile, although silence in this case was relative, they communicated telepathically anyway; let's say that for a few seconds there was nothing else in their minds but an awe inspiring admiration, mixed with at least a dozen other emotions, homesickness being one of them. It was autumn in the northern hemisphere, where they came from, and this filled them with anticipation to see the autumn colours once again and then other desires introduced themselves too. They hastened to say their goodbyes and each of them went their way, excited and hopeful.

It was really comforting to be at home on such a stormy night. It was comforting too that the children were enjoying better weather at her sister's in the South of France. They were having a Halloween party and only work had prevented her from being there with them. But she was due to join them in a day or so for a well-deserved holiday. André was there too, she'd just spoken to him and he'd said that they were all having such fun and wasn't it a shame that she wasn't with them. But employers are not a reasonable lot, at least her's wasn't and the times of family values had long since passed, so she had to content herself with the "quality time" maxim, nod her head and get on with her tasks.

She was very tired by the time she'd finished her long day and was glad to be at home and to get to bed early. She tried to read for a while but it was not for long. She wasn't sure afterwards when exactly she fell asleep. Then she had this rather weird dream.

"It had to be a dream," she was saying later to André, "though at the time it seemed so very real to me."

She woke up, or so she thought, in the middle of the night, with the storm still raging outside and the sleep still in her eyes. There was somebody in her bed, stroking her hair and at first she thought it was André till she realised it couldn't be him, he was miles away, and besides, she knew André so well so that even in the darkness she was sure it wasn't him no matter that her back was turned towards her uninvited visitor. Then she recognised him, it was her husband, but that could not be, for he had lain in a coma for 10 years now. She was speechless for a moment.

"Don't scream," said her husband gently, "it's really me."

"I am not in the habit of screaming as you should well know by now and it's not you anyway, you are in hospital," she was surprised at the logical way her mind was working, "I am just dreaming of course; I will wake up in a minute and say to myself that it's just another bloody nightmare."

"A nightmare to find yourself in bed with your own husband? You used to say that you loved me!"

"So I did, François, so I did, but you didn't deserve it. One fine day, after a weekend with your mistress, you had a car crash and you ended up in hospital, in a coma and I had to manage as well as I could; and bring the children up too."

"I know and you did a terrific job, Jéromine!"

"Your irony is lost on me," she sat up and adjusted the pillow behind her back, "what do you want?"

"I'm not being ironic, I really do appreciate what you did. But why this hostility towards me, what have I done? It's not because of your boyfriend, is it?"

"It's ten years since we've been together, François. I had a lot of time to mull things over. To reflect on your past affaires, your disloyalty and unreliability and your total lack of integrity."

"Wow, there are a lot of big words there, mon chère Jéromine! You did not mind my affaires in the past, you forgave me, you said so yourself. You were crazy about me, you used to say that you could not live without me, remember?"

"I will not deny that. But I was young, naïve and inexperienced at the time, you took advantage of me. And that wasn't fair. We were not meant to be together if you ask me. We are so different in the end. We don't have anything in common."

"But, chérie, I can't believe you are being so harsh with me. We had such fun, remember? All those unforgettable moments? You must have been happy at the time! I did make you happy, don't you dare to deny it!"

"François, what do you expect from me? Why are you here, anyway? You should be in the hospital, how did you get out of there?"

"Ma chérie, I want to be back home. I'll change, I promise you! I'll mend my ways! We'll start a new life together, a better life, you, me and the kids, you have no idea how much I have missed you all!"

"Oh, François, I find this really hard…"

"If you mean your boyfriend, I know all about him but don't worry. I had to arrange a few things in order to find you here alone. I forgive you, really I do. It's only human; we all have our little weaknesses. But you'll be all mine from now on. You belong to me! And I wanted you so much and for so long!"

"No! You are hurting me, François! Let go, let go!"

She tried in vain to push him away from her.

"And then," she was explaining later to André, "and then he tried to kiss me, we wrestled, I think I banged my head against the edge of the headboard and I don't remember anything after that. Next time I opened my eyes, I was on

99

my own, there were no signs that someone had ever been in the house and if it wasn't for some blood under my nails (I remember scratching him at one point), I would've been absolutely sure that it was just a nightmare."

"But you are not so sure now," said André.

"It's all so strange! Next morning I got this call from the hospital, you know, they told me that he'd passed away that very night. I was quite upset; I felt somehow that if I didn't reject him in my dream, he would've still been alive. And then when I went to see him, there was this scratch on his face. It really made me wonder."

She looked at the big, framed photograph of her late husband. It almost looked like his features were somewhat distorted. But of course she must've imagined it. She had been awoken from a nightmare after all and she was still a bit shaken, but it would be fine from now on. She felt sure about that. She took the picture and put it away in the wardrobe, face down. One has to put away the past once and for all, life goes on!

In another hospital in another town, there was great excitement. One of the coma patients had suddenly come out from their sleep. His wife was at his bedside. She had waited for this moment for years.

"I knew it, I knew it!" she was telling her husband excitedly, "I had this weird dream last night and it was very real. I dreamt that you had come back; you said you missed me so much and we'd be together from now on. It was such a lovely dream and when I woke up, I knew that something wonderful was going to happen! So it was not quite such a surprise when they rang me from the hospital with the news!"

They held hands, grateful to be reunited again.

Leaving Earth once again a few saddened beings were communicating their experiences. They felt utterly and totally rejected, especially bearing in mind that some of their initial group had been successful and were actually given a second chance. The others were condemned to leave for good. It was so sad. Earth looked so lovely and yet so unattainable!

Provence,
November 202x

Sophia looked at the manuscript thoughtfully. A tear was glittering in the corner of her eye, but she didn't wipe it.
"A bit morbid, don't you think?" ventured Adrian.
"Yes, rather," agreed Julian hurriedly, exchanging looks with the prince.
Clearly they didn't know what to make of it, but most importantly didn't like the effect it had had on Sophia. But Sylvia was not happy with their verdict:
"I think it's very good. And judging from the time when it was written, I'm sure she must've had me in mind! All right, I wasn't exactly in a coma, but very nearly so – alive, but not quite. Don't you think so, Adrian?"
"Frankly I don't know what to think. But I was just wondering why didn't she ever publish her work?"
"Why indeed?" echoed Sophia, "why was it that Zara only received recognition posthumously? Her works were in fact published by her son after her death and she is now regarded as a founder of the modern literary style. Stylized, but vivid characters, absorbing dialogue, simple description of environment and nature."

"And presumably you still get royalties, excuse me for asking such a question?" Adrian seemed more curious than contrite for his impertinence.

"Royalties?" Sophia clearly did not understand what he was talking about.

"You know, the sum of money paid to an author (or their heirs) for each copy of their work sold; you must still have this today?"

"Oh, of course, but it doesn't apply for such a distant relationship like mine to Zara's."

"Hmm, but what if it is a grandmother – granddaughter relationship? That will surely work, won't it? It's worth finding that out!"

"Don't be silly, Adrian. I don't care for the money," said Sylvia with a reproachful tone.

"That's because you are so young, my dear, and you are so used to having money when you need it, but it doesn't grow on trees, you know!"

"Now who is the mercantile one, I wonder," Julian remarked ironically, referring to an earlier conversation he had had with the prince.

"What's the matter with you, people?"

Adrian looked round at each of them, exasperated by the complete lack of understanding on the part of his audience:

"It's only fair, isn't it? Why shouldn't Sylvia get what she is entitled to? If you don't claim what's your due, you don't get it and others will appropriate it."

He looked at his fiancée with apprehension.

"At any rate I don't give a toss!" Sylvia replied firmly, "don't you see, Adrian? The most important thing is that Gran's talent however belatedly, was finally recognised!"

"I still don't understand," said Julian, looking daggers at Adrian, "how come she didn't receive recognition in her lifetime?"

"It's difficult to explain..." started Sophia hesitantly, "the times, the trends..."

"There was not enough sex in her novels," Adrian said unexpectedly, "sex is implied but not described and left entirely to the imagination."

"Adrian, you are impossible!" protested Sylvia.

"But that's the case, my dear girl! And don't you start lecturing me with those bourgeois maxims, you've been taught at home. I know about the literature of my time, believe you me!"

Sylvia turned to Sophia, but Sophia just shrugged her shoulders:

"I wouldn't have put it so bluntly, but Adrian is more or less right. That's what I was getting at, the trends as I said. Reality shows were prevalent then; conflict was encouraged by the producers and the public were made to feel and indeed, enjoyed being voyeurs, getting glimpses of the private lives of others at a time when privacy was elevated to a cult. If you couldn't see what was going on behind the blinds of your next door neighbour, you might have the chance to see them on television, where they would voluntarily expose their dirty washing in public and satisfy everybody's curiosity. Describing the sex lives of their leading characters in detail had become the recipe of successful writers to launch bestselling novels."

"My Gran's stories were not like that at all. They were clever, they were witty, they were educational even. But she was not interested in describing moments that she considered intimate," Sylvia shook her head. "If privacy is so important, why is it not respected?"

Julian made a face:

"I remember being compared with a peeping Tom once; just because I dared to look back into the lives of our ancestors."

Sylvia blushed and hastened to explain:

"I didn't mean to offend you or Sophia. It's just that I felt guilty; like reading someone else's letters. You see, for you, Gran is indeed just a distant ancestor, long gone and buried; someone you never knew personally; for me it's different. I feel as if she's gone on a journey somewhere and she could come back any time and be rather displeased about us looking to discover her secrets; or Granddad's secrets. Oh well, it's rather silly, I know, but I can't help it."

Sophia hugged her fondly:

"It's alright. We've all been rather insensitive, haven't we? But it's difficult for me to put myself in your shoes; even impossible I might say. But this is also my family's history. I've always been fascinated by it. And Julian gave me the chance to find out so much more about it. Then you arrived and told us about your time. It's been quite a journey."

THE TIME CAPSULE

"You didn't!"

"Yes, I did!"

"Why haven't you told me this before?"

"Because I had forgotten all about it!"

Sylvia was almost running, pulling Adrian along.

"Come, I'll show you!"

"Wait!" Adrian stopped suddenly and Sylvia almost lost her balance and toppled towards him, her long dark hair brushing against his face. He held her close, almost protectively. They kissed and she asked:

"What's the matter?"

"Nothing. You left me breathless, you little minx! But answer me this: have you told Sophie or Julian about your little secret?"

"No, you are the first one, darling. They have their little secrets, we can have ours," she smiled mischievously.

"I don't think it's very fair somehow," persisted Adrian.

"Oh, we'll tell them later. Yes, I know, they'll be curious, but at the end of the day, I am the one calling the shots."

"I still find it incredible! You actually thought of a time capsule!"

"Not only thought, but went ahead with it and buried it."

"Is it far from here? Slow down a bit, people my age shouldn't be running marathons like this! Besides I am carrying these heavy tools of yours."

"Stuart carried the tools for me at the time. But he was useless with the digging, just wasn't programmed to do it. Come on, we are almost there. People your age are only too keen to run after young girls, or so they say."

Adrian rolled his eyes up but followed her never the less. He knew her well enough to realize that when she'd got a bee under her bonnet, there was no stopping her. Eventually they reached their destination. The place was well chosen: down a slope and quite well hidden from view. A big cypress tree was stretching its green fingers out to the sky. Sylvia had buried her time capsule in its roots all those years ago. Adrian looked around, doubtful:

"Is it still here I wonder?"

"Why not? I shoved the stuff in a stoneware pot, packed it up in bubble wrap and then placed it in a wooden box which I then put in a plastic bag!"

"Hmm, that was clever of you. Plastic lasts for ever."

"While I was sick, they were talking about the Deep Freeze and planning things and I thought then that later on when I was out of it, back amongst the living, I'd like to have a few things preserved as a keepsake, let's say. If something went wrong, well, somebody surely would find it one day, I reasoned, so whatever happened it was going to be fine by me."

"And you came here with this treasure chest of yours and started to dig in the ground?" asked Adrian incredulously.

"Yes. It was harder than I thought. I didn't manage to bury it very deep. But we'll see if its still there. I had forgotten all about it, of course, so many things have happened since. But then I found my Gran's jewellery box in that secret cupboard and it dawned on me that I too had a little cache of my own. I came here this morning and found the tree still standing and the box must be there, under its roots!"

"I see, you are a family of hoarders! Stashing away your valuables in secret places! But let's see what we've got here."

"You have to dig it out, darling. That's the spot, right there," Sylvia pointed with her delicate finger.

"Are you sure?"

"Almost."

"Not quite sure and yet you insist I dig? Don't tell anybody this, please! Don't tell them that you convinced Adrian, a prince of royal blood, to dig in search of buried treasure!"

"It's not exactly a treasure as such, but it's valuable to me! Please, please, Adrian, don't be stubborn! It will be fun."

"It seems everything is fun for you, *mon amie*, but well, I'll do it. When a lady asks a favour, how can I refuse?"

The sun was slipping down below the horizon in a splash of fire-red colours giving a purple lining to all the clouds around. Julian stood near the window to admire it.

"Where have those two disappeared?" asked Sophia, coming out of the dining room, "It's time for dinner. And why have they left the dog behind?"

"They've been out for ages," replied Julian, "but don't worry, they know how to look after themselves. Come to see the sunset."

"It is spectacular," admitted Sophia.

Julian put his arm round her waist and gently pulled her towards him. They stood in silence overwhelmed by the beauty that only nature can create. Finally Sophia said:

"It's getting dark. I'll call them. They might be lost somewhere out there."

"Don't be silly! What could possibly happen? They can call us if they are in trouble. Let them be! They are young and they need some privacy."

But Sophia called them anyway.

"Their communicators are switched off," she said.

"Predictable! What else did you expect?"

"I don't like it, Julian. Come, I'll track them down."

"Sophie, don't start panicking. I am sure they are fine."

"You know damn well, Julian, that the Adapt Centre is tracking them constantly anyway. The team there knows their whereabouts at any given moment. I should've cautioned those young fools about this earlier. If they are up to something dodgy…"

Julian was shaking his head in disapproval while they were looking at the big screen that was currently displaying a detailed map of the grounds and part of the surrounding area. "There they are," he said pointedly, "coming this way. I told you to be more patient, you won't listen."

"You know, Julian, things have changed for me in recent times. Before I didn't mind being watched at all times, for I had nothing to hide. My conscience was clear. Not that I feel like a criminal now, but as we are in possession of certain information that has to be kept secret, I don't want any attention drawn towards us."

"I told you not to worry on that score. I always activate a protective sound shield around us, so our conversations cannot be overheard. Give me some credit there, my dear! I've been extremely careful since, since…but that's another story, we won't talk about it."

"But why not? Can't you trust me?"

"Of course I can trust you. But it's better this way. The less you know, the better. Here they come our young lovers, tell them off! You see both are safe and sound."

"And very disappointed," added Sylvia with a sigh, taking off her muddy boots, "I was sure I buried it there, but it's gone!"

"What have you buried? What's gone?" asked Sophia in alarm.

"My time capsule!"

"What are you talking about, child?"

"Apparently, Sylvia had buried a time-capsule at some point during the period of her illness, just before she was consigned to the Deep Freeze, in fact. She put some knick-knacks in it and when she was reminded of its existence, she dragged me all the way down there," Adrian, grinning like a Cheshire cat, motioned in the direction where they had just come from, "she dragged me with her kicking and screaming to help her to retrieve it. But it wasn't there anymore. Someone must've found it already."

"Oh!" Sophia was noticeably relieved, "was that all? I wondered what you were up to. You left the robot behind and the dog; I tell you Rufus is not impressed with you at all! And for what? To dig in my back yard! And, by the way, you are late for dinner!"

Later that evening Adrian lounged back in his armchair and looked at Sylvia:

"So what was hidden in that cache of yours? Diamonds?"

"Of course not! Just a few bits and pieces, as you suggested. Let me think. A no-smoking plaque my cousin had nicked from a pub in Windsor, a little polar bear figurine, that dad had brought me from Alaska, a paper weight featuring a nice sea landscape, that came from nanny after a holiday in Portugal, a little broach of a horse that I used to wear, a Russian doll from Gran and Granddad when they returned from Moscow..."

"Was that all? Much ado about nothing, I'd say! Look at my hands, look at the blisters I've got and for what? For a no-smoking sign which wasn't even there! Stuart!"

"Yes, sir!"

"She dragged you there too, didn't she?"

"Who dragged me where, sir?"

"Sylvia dragged you with her to carry her tools and help her bury her treasure chest!"

"Yes, sir!"

"So you can find the spot where it's buried."

"Yes I can, sir, but the box is not there any more."

"Of course it's not, you fool! Somebody must have found it."

"Yes, sir. The gardener."

"The gardener?"

"The gardener asked me what we were playing about at, digging under the trees and I answered that mistress had buried a box there."

"What did he say?"

"He said: "Bloody children and their silly games, treasure hunts and what not!"

"And then what? Then he dug it up and gave it to Master. Master said: "Put it in the loft, Stuart." And I did."

Sylvia was looking at the robot in disbelief:

"Why didn't you tell me, Stuart?"

"You didn't ask, mistress."

"There is perfect logic for you, darling! You didn't ask, he didn't tell you. Look at him, he appears downright smug about it."

"So the box is probably still in the loft then," pursued Sylvia.

"Probably. But I am not rushing to search for it now. It has waited all this time; it can wait till tomorrow."

In her bedroom Sophia was thoughtfully combing her hair in front of the mirror. Julian was standing behind her and their eyes met.

"Tell me," she said pleadingly, "you were going to, weren't you?"

"I was, but then I changed my mind. You don't want to know, believe me."

"Try me!"

"Alright. I'd better. Where shall I start from? Once upon a time I had a friend, a colleague, the one who actually started all this research, which I later pursued and brought to completion. He died in an accident. Something allegedly had happened to his antigrav, a technical failure of some sort or another, they say, which, you have to admit is extremely rare these days. I gained access to his findings later, after receiving a few words from him saying if something ever happened to him (and if I got that note then that time must've come), I had to continue with his research but keep it absolutely secret. Which is exactly what I did. Everybody thinks I am still working on an abstract project which won't have any practical application. I was going to publish my findings, but on reflection, I considered it too dangerous."

"You told me, we can change neither the past nor the future," Sophia reminded him.

"We can't. But there are always unscrupulous people, crooks and such, who might use my invention for some dubious practices. And what bothers me most is the death of my friend. I keep wondering. Was it really an accident? Maybe somebody out there was after him? Trying to get hold of his research perhaps? Or trying to destroy it? And what if they were to find out that I have made a breakthrough? Yes, I know it might sound like paranoia, but...and as you said yourself we really do live in a Big Brother reality, when you are aware that all the time someone, somewhere is watching you and you don't know who and you don't know why. Sometimes it really gets to me."

"I know, Julian, I know. I understand."

She was silent for awhile but then she added almost as an afterthought:

"When my late husband perished in that dreadful accident, I wanted to know the truth, I badly wanted to know it. Something had gone terribly wrong there and I just had to find out whose fault it was. But then I was told by certain parties to keep out of it if I valued my own life. It was obvious by then that someone influential was at the bottom of it all. I wondered whether it was carefully planned sabotage or simply negligence as a result of trying to cut costs. I'll never know. I did some research on the Net; you know that I have almost unlimited access there these days, but all the secret files connected with this case had simply disappeared; just gone. Isn't that significant? It seems that I am not to find the truth - ever."

Julian looked at her hesitantly:

"I don't know how to say this but I want to put your mind at rest. It was an accident. As you rightly assumed, the company was trying to cut costs and the materials used were cheap and nasty. I suppose you've heard about metal fatigue? That was the main reason for the catastrophe. Add to it some malfunctioning monitors, also cheap and unreliable, and you have the whole picture. The directors involved managed to keep themselves out of the limelight. They had pocketed huge amounts of credit in the form of bonuses and they bribed their way out of responsibility."

Sophia was staring at him with incredulity, hairbrush still in her hand:

"How on earth do you know all this? In the official version it was stated that small technical failures had occurred coincidently at the same time as human error, all contributing to result in such a terrible outcome. My husband was implicated for negligence, although not directly. I found this hard to believe. He was an excellent pilot with a lot of experience, always a stickler for procedures. From what you are telling me it appears that he was entirely blameless in this matter as I've always maintained. But how come you know so much about this accident and have you got any evidence?"

"Well, I was one of the expert witnesses called to give a verdict as to the causes of the catastrophe. I wrote a report which it seems was not taken into account when closing the case. When I enquired about the reasons for disregarding it, I was told that I had done my job and to leave the rest to the courts. I would not let it go, but as I persisted, I found my whole livelihood threatened; I was told that the funds I was counting on to complete the research I was doing at the time, were unlikely to be disbursed. Much as I wanted to be a hero, I have to admit that at that point I just gave up. This was the time when I got involved in the "bubble-theory", inherited from my friend. In fact if it wasn't for his death, I would've probably persevered on the space catastrophe front by making my report public with God only knows what consequences. The fate of my friend sobered me. He had also received various threats, I know that for sure, but he carried on regardless, which, sadly, led to his untimely demise."

"Julian! Why haven't you told me all this before?"

"How could I? You've never spoken to me about these things, not till now. I didn't dare to broach the subject, I didn't want to upset you. Our relationship, so precious to me, is still I feel, quite fragile. You retire every now and then behind a wall of silence. I don't know what you are thinking or how you feel. You might not care much for me, but I know that I don't want to lose you."

Sophia left her hairbrush on the dressing table and held her hands palms up towards him:

"But Julian, it's precisely because I care for you that I didn't want to burden you with my emotional turmoil. I am sorry you took it the wrong way."

Julian tenderly wiped the tears from her eyes and took her in his arms:

"It's all right, it's all right."

He was lost for words.

"You could've told me all this when we first met," Sophia remarked, smiling through her tears, "it would've been easier, and excuse enough to approach me."

"I thought about it," admitted Julian, "but I could not bring myself to do it. It was known how depressed you were after what you had been through and I felt it would've been monstrous of me to have you again experience all those painful moments. You looked so vulnerable, so tragically beautiful; the mere idea of taking advantage of the circumstances to further my plans, upsetting you in the process, made me feel the villain, it cut me right to the quick. I wasn't proud of myself for even considering such a thing."

113

"I think, I can now close that page of my life and leave it to rest," whispered Sophia after awhile, pressing Julian's hand. "I now realise how this unfinished quest for the truth was preventing me from carrying on with the rest of my life. At one stage I wanted vengeance. But now I know that one should not let oneself be consumed by hatred. Life is too short anyway so it is essential to forgive in order that I can get on with it. But I won't forget. If it were not for so many happy memories to dwell upon, it probably would not be worth living at all. At least nobody can take them away from me."

After a few more minutes she added:

"Your time capsule, Julian, had a far greater effect, I think than the one Sylvia was looking for, far greater I am sure than you could've imagined. And it wasn't revealed a moment too soon."

IN THE ATTIC

"That's impossible," Sylvia thought, "that's truly a Herculean task!"

She was standing in the attic, looking around her in dismay. The attic of her childhood had been relatively tidy and a favourite haunt of hers at the time, a place where she felt she was moving into a mysterious and magical world; it had since become an ungovernable and seemingly overgrown jungle. Was that possible? Was this the same space at all or had it been altered, like so many things, to the point of becoming almost unrecognisable?

She looked at the ceiling: exposed beams, darkened with age, a couple of skylights letting in some sunlight to penetrate the dark recesses of this depository. The ceiling at least looked the same notwithstanding the ravages of time; as for the rest – well, it was probably also unchanged as far as the construction was concerned; it was just overflowing with junk accumulated over the years, the junk of many generations, never cleared, never sorted out, forgotten.

"So what do you expect me to do?" asked Adrian impatiently, "it will be like looking for a needle in a haystack! Anyway, your box might be there or might not be. Going through other people's belongings is not exactly my idea of having fun. I have enough at home to deal with."

"Please, please, Rip, you have to help me! I am sure my time capsule is somewhere here, sitting in a dark corner, waiting to be retrieved..."Sylvia pleaded.

"Let's go for a walk, let's go for a walk!" insisted Rufus, desperate to be out.

"You see, Rufus has different ideas," remarked Adrian.

"He can wait for half an hour or so!"

"Half an hour! You must be joking! You said yourself there is an enormous amount of stuff to sift through! Yesterday you were absolutely convinced that the blooming thing was buried under that tree, but as it turned out... "

Sylvia bit her lip. She knew when she was beaten. Yet she made a final effort to persuade Adrian:

"It will be like a treasure hunt, won't it? You have no idea what might be hidden in there!"

"Let's go for a walk, let's go, let's go," persisted Rufus.

"Coming, my boy," replied Adrian soothingly and then, turning to Sylvia, "I wouldn't expect much if I were you; people don't store anything of value in attics. Whatever is up here is just junk, mark my words, it is going to be fit only for the rubbish tip."

Whistling to Rufus, Adrian walked out of the front door, leaving a perplexed Sylvia behind him.

She tiptoed to Julian's laboratory. Julian was busy. He didn't even hear her coming, so engrossed was he in an experiment that he was conducting.

"Julian!"

"Yes! Blimey! What the hell is going on here? Can you check those readings for me, Sylvie? Thank you! I don't understand, I don't understand, that's not right! Ah-hah! That must be the reason why I am getting this nonsense!"

He bent over his calculations, shaking his head. Sylvia left him to get on with it. She went in search of Sophia, though she didn't expect much from her either. Most likely she would find her no less busy than Julian. Sophia was about to finish a historical book she had been writing for a long time; it was about events that had happened in the past, but at a time when Sylvia was still in the Deep Freeze and about which she knew nothing. To Sophia's great consternation she was not in the slightest interested in them.

"What if I ask her about her work and then encourage her to have a little rest," wondered Sylvia, "this might just do the trick? It's worth a try."

When Sylvia entered Sophia's study, she found her standing in front of the French windows, seemingly admiring the view.

"Have you got a minute?" asked Sylvia tentatively.

Sophia turned round and smiled:

"Maybe. It depends."

"It's about the attic," Sylvia pursued her thought, "I went to have a look and was shocked to find it so cluttered. How on Earth have you let it get into such a condition? And how do you find anything there?"

Sylvia pretended to be rather outraged in the hope of enlisting Sophia's assistance. It worked better than she expected.

"Oh, well," replied Sophia sheepishly, "you know how it is. One lets things get out of hand and then it's too difficult to remedy them. I personally don't go up there very often and what's there now is more or less what I've inherited, so to speak. But perhaps you are right," pursued Sophia after a pause, talking more to herself than to Sylvia, "perhaps now is as good a time as any to have a look there and clear the stuff. No doubt there will be a lot of stuff that needs sorting out and getting rid of. Mind you, it's going to be an arduous task. We need to get some help."

"I spoke to Adrian, but he is not very keen to be involved in it. He said he had enough rubbish of his own to sort out…"

"Never mind what he says," replied Sophia, who had obviously made up her mind, "I'll talk to him. Let's go up there and make a preliminary study of the situation before starting the task in earnest."

Sunlight was streaming through the skylights, specs of dust were dancing in the air. Sophia walked down the narrow path purposefully left between lines of boxes arranged along the walls.

"I think it is somewhere around here," she said, "ah, this must be it. Come and have a look, Julian."

"It" was a small panel fixed to the wall that had some push buttons and a joy-stick on it. Julian scrutinised it carefully.

"Well, it's pretty simple really. Let's give it a try," he stated eventually, pushing one of the buttons.

Some old machinery woke up. There were certain loud, grating and squeaking sounds and then along a metal pole fixed to the ceiling slid a metal gizmo equipped with steel arms designed for holding and lifting.

"But that's ingenious! Every house should have one!" exclaimed Adrian, craning his neck upwards, "who would've thought?"

"Yeah, but you had to be dragged here kicking and screaming to see it," Sylvia remarked in an unforgiving tone. "Mark my words," she pursued, trying not very successfully to mimic Adrian's voice, "mark my words, all you will find here will be just rubbish!"

"All right, all right," replied Adrian in a conciliatory tone, *"mea culpa."*

"So you are saying, it was your grand-uncle, Sophie, who came up with this contraption?" asked Julian.

"Yes. I don't remember him, of course, he died before I was even born, but I've heard a lot about him. He was my grandfather's elder brother. Remained a bachelor all his life and a bit of a hermit. All he cared for were his inventions. There are some technical drawings of his, kept in the family archive to prove how talented he was and how eccentric. An excellent draughtsman, he wouldn't use a computer, but did everything by hand! What a waste of time!"

"The crazy inventor in the attic?"

"I am afraid so. But this contraption of his is going to come in handy now, don't you think?"

"Indeed! But let's get this box down. There it goes!"

The box was duly lifted and lowered down exactly in front of them, thanks to Julian's skill in manipulating the joy-stick.

"It's even labelled!" remarked Sylvia, "obviously there was somebody in this family who was tidy and organised."

"It was my father," replied Sophia, "and if this label is correct, "we'll find his drawings inside. Right! Here they are! This is exciting! I've seen some of them scanned and stored in the family archive, but these are the originals. I had no idea that they kept them. Apparently he was talented, but did not pursue it, he went into geology instead. Look at this! It's a sketch of the façade of "Elounda". Judging by the date, it must've been done when he was 11 years old. It's good, isn't it?"

An hour later and a few more boxes further on, Sylvia noticed a little case in a corner. She rushed over and opened it before Sophia had the chance to stop her. There was a uniform there and a pair of boots.

"Ah!" Sylvia was disappointed, "Whose is this uniform?"

"It's Jason's," replied Sophia calmly, "my late husband. I've disposed of his clothes, but kept the uniform. But it's time for it to go at last. I now know the truth and the whole matter should be laid to rest."

"The truth?" inquired Adrian.

"The truth about the accident. Tell them, Julian."

"About the accident," Julian cleared his throat, "there wasn't any sabotage involved. By trying to cut costs in using cheap materials, the company concerned was responsible for the death toll that took place, but instead of facing up to the consequences of that, they tried to lay the blame on the pilot, on Jason Leonard, Sophia's husband."

"I didn't handle the media very well, I am afraid," added Sophia ruefully, "but they just wouldn't leave me alone. They wanted to show to the world the grieving widow of the pilot guilty for the accident, but instead, I appeared very composed in front of them and announced that my husband was the victim of either sabotage or else somebody's negligence and they had better find out who the guilty party really was instead of distressing me. It didn't go down very well."

"Yes, I remember the headlines: "WIDOW OF EARTH-MARS KILLER-PILOT POINTS FINGER TO UNKNOWN GUILTY PARTY, SAYS HUBBY DIDN'T DO IT.""

"It was awful," continued Sophia, "there were even insinuations that Jason was under the influence of alcohol during that fatal trip. I remember being asked if he was teetotal and I replied that he was not, but so what? In the article following that, it was stated: "WIDOW ADMITS THAT HUSBAND HAD A DRINK PROBLEM". One reporter actually told me, confidentially, that they were instructed to stir it up along those lines. He didn't want to lose his job and cautioned me to be careful in my determination to discover the truth."

"But you had the last word, didn't you?" said Julian.

"I had had enough of reporters by then. I got in touch with the Organisation for Protection of Human Rights and Privacy and lodged a complaint. I got an injunction according to which they were banned from coming near my person or even on my estate, in whatever circumstances, unless explicitly invited by me. And that was that. I was finally left alone."

Adrian and Sylvia listened to these revelations in silence.

"You are a real hero, Sophie," said Sylvia eventually, "an unsung hero."

"Is there ever a sung hero, I wonder?" Adrian was clearly trying to lighten the conversation a bit, but then he added almost as an afterthought, "the bastards, I hope they get what they deserve."

"Oh, they will," said Julian with conviction, "sooner or later. Nothing goes unpunished. I've deposited my evidence on the E-Lawyers database and it's going to be automatically opened after my death. I can't do anything more at the moment, because they'll prevent me, but one day…"

"Nobody who knew Jason believed in those shenanigans in any case," said Sophia. "I have since been contacted by so many people, who offered me their help and support. It was important for me to know the truth."

She closed the trunk and attempted a smile:

"This chapter is now closed."

APPARITION FROM THE FUTURE

The day happened to be overcast and grey. Autumn was in the air, as evidenced by strong gusts of wind, driving black rainy clouds across the sky. Darkness descended early, exacerbated by the stormy weather, chasing Sylvie, Adrian and Rufus, the setter home ahead of time. Approaching "Elounda" they rounded the corner and suddenly became aware of its dark silhouette looming above them. The lighting should've switched on automatically at dusk but it hadn't. They saw a flickering light inside but for some inexplicable reason, an irrational fear seized them and they hesitated whether to enter or not. The front door was suddenly flung open and the light directed towards them momentarily blinded them.

"Oh, you are back at long last!" exclaimed a familiar voice.

Adrian passed a trembling hand over his brow:

"What on Earth is going on, Sophie?"

"I wish I knew. Malfunction of some sort. Julian is trying to sort things out, for it was one of his experiments that caused the lights to go out in the first instance."

"It's scary," said Sylvia, "a stormy night outside, the whole place plunged into darkness, not to mention that we've just been stalked by a horrid old man."

"An old man?" asked Sophia.

"Yeah, he looked like a beggar, wearing rags and..."

"Ah, that's old Mario, he lives in a dilapidated old house not far from here; the last survivor of an old family. He is harmless, I assure you, just curious I guess. But what is Julian doing? He said that it wouldn't take him a minute to fix the problem, but he's been gone for ages keeping us waiting here in the dark. Julian? What are you doing?"

As if as a response to this call, the lights came back to life, but then flickered and the entrance where the three of them were still standing, was plunged into darkness once more. Well, not entirely. A luminescent glow twinkled in front of their dismayed eyes, taking the shape of a ghostly figure, wearing a toga like garment. Nobody uttered a word; they just stood there, staring. Julian who had joined them at the same moment was likewise affected. Rufus was growling, clearly confused for even his voice emitter didn't convey his emotions into words as usual. Meanwhile, the apparition tried to communicate with them, for they saw the movement of its (his) lips, but whatever was said was inaudible. It or he then waved its (his) hands in resignation and disappeared. The lights came on simultaneously.

Adrian was the first one to move:
"What the hell was that?" and, noticing Julian amongst them, turned on him, "blimey! Some of us might've suffered a heart attack as a result of this silly prank you played on us. I don't find it funny at all!"

But Julian appeared concerned rather than amused. He looked around in a perplexed fashion, shaking his head.
"I can't understand it at all. This shouldn't have happened. It's not possible, unless, unless…"
"Unless what?" asked Sophia impatiently, "tell us, Julian, don't keep us in suspense."
"I have to think this through. I'll check what the readings of my instruments say, that is, if they are still working. But it seems almost like…no, that's just impossible, the energy it requires…no wonder the lights went off."
He hurried towards his laboratory leaving them to recover from the shock.
"I wonder what he has in mind," ventured Sophia, "naturally I was flabbergasted like you when this ghost suddenly materialised in front of us and then vanished into thin air as they say, but then I thought of something that Julian once said a long time ago. It was about these time-bubbles of his. If I am not mistaken, he said he believed that in them time goes both ways and there was a pretty good chance that one

123

would encounter not ghosts of course, but just people who lived a long time ago."

"Ghosts *are* people who lived a long time ago," remarked Sylvia.

Still shaken by the recent events, she tried to appear nonchalant, but didn't really fool anybody. For a start, all the colour had drained from her face and she was convulsively pressing Adrian's hand, who, for his part, decided it fell to him to ease the tension and alleviate the ladies' fears:

"So, the house is haunted then," he said lightly, "it befits an old mansion like this one to have its own resident ghost. But why are we still standing here? Aren't you going to invite us in, Sophie? I wouldn't mind having a drink, preferably a strong one, have you got any brandy?"

"Of course!" replied Sophia mechanically, still deep in thought, trying to recall what Julian had said at the time about the time-bubbles. She was not good at physics and had difficulty grasping the whole concept of the space/time continuum despite Julian's explanations.

They headed for the so-called drawing room. Each of the rooms in the house was furnished in a different style, reflecting the changes in fashion during its long period of almost continuous occupation since it came into existence in the 20th century. The drawing room was the only one that had been left more or less intact, its colour scheme, decorative elements, furnishings and furniture in a style more in tune with a sumptuous Palladian villa, rather than with the rustic simplicity of the typical Provençal villa, that "Elounda" was intended to be. And yet the overall effect was stunning, the room itself taking you into a time warp in its own right.

Sylvia's grandmother Zara, who had painstakingly conceived each and every detail and then oversaw the work, completed by skilled local craftsmen from start to finish, had indeed succeeded in creating a space where someone from the Renaissance would not have felt out of place. The frescos on the walls, allegories from ancient Greek mythology, all were executed by a talented artist, a friend of Philip. It was said that one of the muses, Calliope, depicted in profile, was in fact Zara herself, who was alleged to have inspired the artist and rumoured also to have broken his heart. How much of that was true, was anybody's guess. According to some sources, the artist was actually gay and that was the real reason why he'd never married.

The other question in connection with the room, that Sophia and presumably lots of others were puzzled about, was why on earth had Zara gone to all this trouble, doing this particular room up, in such a contrast with the rest of its surroundings. It was Sylvia who finally explained the mystery. Zara was apparently a woman with a great sense of humour, amongst her other qualities. She had married a successful architect, sought out by a lot of rich and influential people, who were showering him with commissions. Zara and Philip were entertaining a lot at their new house and the drawing/reception room was designed to appeal to his nouveau riche patrons. She had correctly gauged their taste (or lack of it) and had provided the right atmosphere for their visits, without compromising her own set standards, in this splendid room that never failed to impress.

This was the room that our trio had entered and were now relaxing on the sofas, lovingly restored by Sophia to their former glory, sipping the cognac she had poured into their glasses.

"I give you this, Sophie, despite the fall in standards in your time, you have managed to keep yours up, at least as far as your cellar is concerned. I haven't tasted such a good vintage since I went into the Deep Freeze. On the eve of my departure, a friend of mine brought me a...well, let's say a farewell gift, a bottle of Courvoisier. We drank most of it that evening. I asked my brother to keep what remained for me to finish when I returned...if ever. Much to my surprise, he did. It was kept in the family vault in the bank. On my release from the Adapt Centre I finished it off, although sadly it had largely evaporated no matter that he'd carefully corked it. Alas, it just didn't taste the same, so the first drink I had in my new life was a bit of a disappointment. I thought at the time that my taste buds must've lost their sensitivity, but perhaps not."

"No, it doesn't seem so," said Sylvia who had now recovered from her shock and was not in the slightest interested in Adrian's drinking exploits. "I wouldn't worry about your taste buds if I were you, but about the unexplained appearance of this ghost. It's not even Halloween today, is it?"

"That would've been the limit if it was!" Adrian chuckled, "Sophie, you were saying something about "bubbles"..."

"It's Julian's theory, the theory of "time-bubbles". Unfortunately I am out of my depth there. He was telling me things about time being like a river..."

"A river that meanders along," Julian finished her sentence, as he entered the room, "that's the space/time continuum; it does not go in a straight line though we might perceive it that way."

"Does it mean then that sometimes it goes back on itself, moving for a little while parallel to an earlier section of its course?" Sylvia was trying in vain to visualise this really abstract notion.

"It's actually rather like a sphere, if we want to be more precise, but let's not complicate things further."

"Perhaps a ball of thread is a more accurate comparison then?" Sylvia persisted doggedly.

"If you like," Julian said impatiently. "Anyway, to put it in a nutshell, a time-bubble is a phenomenon that gives us a chance to witness events that had happened in the past, or will happen in the future by projecting pure consciousness in time. I am afraid I can't explain it clearer than that."

"But how is it possible to see as far back as that?" asked Sylvia, "The man we saw was undoubtedly Roman."

"Why do you think he was Roman?" Julian looked surprised.

"Because he was wearing a toga!"

"True, but his hairstyle was far too elaborate for that period, and besides, he was also wearing a watch," countered Sophia.

"Oh! Are you sure it was a watch and not some sort of a bracelet?"

"If it wasn't exactly a watch, it must've been some fancy gadget or other, that only a more advanced civilisation could produce," Julian stated, "I have reasons to believe, that our visitor came from the future."

"The future!" echoed Sophia, "Are you sure?"

"Quite sure. My instruments confirm it."

It was a bright sunny morning and nobody was yet awake when Sylvia sneaked out of the house and headed toward the sea. She knew that Sophia would object strongly to such behaviour, but she didn't care. Adrian was away for a day or two and she felt restless. Besides what could possibly happen? She had got used to the idea now of being watched at all times and although she did not like it at all, this gave her the comfort of feeling protected.

Down a narrow path, she finally reached the coast. A wide pedestrian bridge – partly escalator, partly - travelator arched over a busy road to take her to the sea. The beach was further away, Sylvia found herself amidst a vast expanse of rocky formations, a favourite spot of hers since childhood. She sat down to admire the view. The sea was way down below and she could smell its salty breath. She inhaled deeply with pleasure. A movement behind her made her brusquely turn round, just in time to face the old man who had scared her a couple of days earlier. She screamed.

Back in the house Sophia was preparing breakfast in the kitchen.

"I wish she wouldn't pull stunts like that!" she said irritably to Julian, who stood beside her, drinking his coffee.

"You worry far too much," he replied, "I am sure she can take good care of herself. Give her some space and don't fuss like a mother hen. Besides it's Adrian who should fret over his fiancée's little escapades, not you."

"The sooner they get married, the better!" said Sophia flatly.

Julian put his cup down on the counter and looked at her:

"Ah, that's quite a turn, I can't actually believe I am hearing this! What made you change your mind all of a sudden?"

She sighed, brushing a strand of hair with the back of her hand away from her eyes before confessing:

"Frankly, I find the responsibility too much for me. It really, really wears me down. You say, I worry too much. I do. I know I shouldn't, but that's the way it is, and I can't do anything about it. When they get married, as you rightly pointed out, it's Adrian who will have to take on this responsibility. I would feel relieved then. And, I have to admit, he is going to cope a lot better than me."

"Yeah, Adrian is a decent fellow. And he is usually quite laid back and relaxed, unless he bumps into a ghost of one sort or another. Then he does get really scared stiff. Ha! Can you actually bump into them I wonder? Perhaps you wouldn't feel any obstruction at all, you would just be on the other side before you even knew it."

"Julian, you come up with the most bizarre notions at times! Going right through a ghost! Brrr! The mere thought makes me shiver! What do you think he wanted from us, that ghost of yours?"

"Why do you think he had anything to do with me?"

"Why did he appear exactly during your experiment? Don't you find it too much of a coincidence?"

"Yeah, I suppose the timing was meticulous," Julian admitted, "but perhaps he had to."

"How do you mean?"

"Well, he used the energy produced from my experiment, didn't he? In fact he needed even more than that, so he used all he could get from any source available and that's why he left us in the dark."

"Oh! But I still don't understand why did he come at all. What was his purpose?" Sophia insisted, "was he looking for somebody in particular? Or perhaps the people from the future are so bored that they amuse themselves with time travel in order to spice up their lives a bit?"

"Perhaps. Or perhaps he just wanted to tell us something. I distinctly saw his lips moving."

Julian was pensive for a moment or two. Then it seemed that he had made his mind up:

"Tell you what. Why don't I reset the whole experiment again and see what happens? But this time we'll have to do it during the day or think about alternative light sources if it's dark. What do you say?"

Sophia was shaking her head in disbelief:

"You are crazy, Julian! And yet that's what I mostly like about you, since the first time we met, and that most extraordinary way you introduced yourself to me. You just came into my life, there and then, without warning, without even giving me time to adjust to what was coming."

"Do you regret it then?" Julian asked archly.

"What do you think? Am I likely to regret the best thing that has happened to me in the last few years?" she said and then added "not now!" pushing Julian's hand away the moment he had started to unbutton her blouse, "I think Sylvia is back."

Sylvia entered the room and looked hesitantly around to gauge the atmosphere. Then reassured, she reached for the coffee.

"Well?" asked Julian, "aren't you going to say hello and tell us what you've been up to? We feared you might've been kidnapped by evil forces, or that ghost from the other night."

Sylvia tossed her hair back:

"You are not that far from the truth."

"What?!" Sophia almost dropped her toast, "what do you mean?"

"Maybe not exactly an encounter with a ghost, but the experience was scary enough. I was sort of accosted by that old man, Mario, when I was down by the sea. I thought: that's it, I am being punished for my disobedience…"

"What happened next?" asked Sophia relieved.

"The weirdest thing. Mario is quite nice actually, just a bit batty. He gave me this photo, look!"

"Gosh! That's you with Zara and a young girl! Amazing!"

"It is, isn't it? I couldn't believe my eyes when I saw it. You see, this is my *nounou* here (nanny Annie as we used to call her) with Gran and me. I must've been six or so at the time."

All three of them looked at the faded photograph. It was a charming picture, taken presumably somewhere in the grounds on a sunny day. Zara was sitting on a white wooden bench, wearing a broad straw hat so her face was in shade, she looked quite youthful; next to her nanny Annie, in shorts, laughing merrily, displaying an immaculate set of pearly white teeth; the child Sylvia was standing in front, leaning on her nanny's knees and looking quizzically up towards her grandmother, her face in profile slightly tilted back, strands of unruly hair coming out from her ponytail. It was a pity that the artist friend of Zara and Philip had not depicted this delightful little scene in an oil painting. But somebody else had captured it on camera, and it wasn't surprising that it had been framed and treasured. Faded as it was, it still had the same appeal it must have had at the time.

"But how come he's got this picture? It's nicely framed, this is silver, I believe; not withstanding the ravages of time, it would look almost new if we cleaned it up. It was obviously a treasured possession, but whose?" asked Julian, putting into words the question on everybody's mind.

"Well, it seems clear to me that there are not that many possibilities," declared Sylvia, "I remember two of those photos, both identically framed. One stood on Gran's night table, the other – on nanny's chest of drawers."

"And who was that mysterious nanny of yours?" asked Julian with interest.

"She was a local girl," replied Sylvia, "she lived with us for awhile and I was very fond of her. Later on she got married, but as I was a lot older by that time, she was never replaced, not in the house, not in our hearts either."

"Oh, that's sweet," said Sophia, "this photo might've been hers then. Did she remain in the area?"

"Oh yes! She came to visit us very often after her marriage. But why do you ask that?"

"I have a hunch. But let me check something first. And you, young lady, you must have your breakfast now, not just coffee!"

Sophia left the room and did not return for some time, an interval, which Sylvia employed by telling Julian all sorts of amusing stories about her nanny Annie.

"She must've been quite an angel this Annie, to put up with a little horror like you," remarked Julian.

"If I was that bad, she wouldn't have been so upset at leaving us," replied Sylvia in the same joking tone, "unless…unless she had her reasons. Sometimes I thought that she had a crush on Daddy. But perhaps I was imagining things, for I was reading "Jane Eyre" at the time."

"Jane Eyre?"

"Oh, I forgot you wouldn't know anything about it. It's a book written by an English novelist, a woman by the name of Charlotte Bronte and it's about a nanny who had an affair with her employer; they were to get married (for in those times people had to be married to live together), but horror of horrors, it turned out that he was already married to a crazy woman, kept under lock and key in the attic!"

"Oh dear! Surely that wasn't suitable reading material for a child! How come this novel was not in that hidden cupboard stacked with all the books you were banned from looking at?"

"How should I know? Daddy didn't object; I heard him saying it was a good puritanical work, teaching a girl how to resist temptation, whatever that means."

"And you are saying your nanny might've been enamoured of such a man?" Julian asked incredulously.

Sylvia shrugged her shoulders, with an expression on her face implying that she knew more than she'd admitted:

"As I said, I was probably just imagining things."

Sophia reappeared with a big smile on her face:

"Guess what?"

"What?" Julian and Sylvia asked simultaneously.

"Old Mario is in fact a descendant of your nanny, he is one of her great-great-grandsons!"

"Isn't that amazing!" exclaimed Sylvia, "how did you find out? Ah, but why do I ask, when I know you have such an infinite source of information at your fingertips?"

"Why indeed? But it was quite easy actually," replied Sophia in a business-like tone, "it took me some time, of course, but it was worth it. I checked Mario's origins, it was all in the database, and then I looked for his female ancestry at that particular period of time when you were a child; then I crosschecked, searching for a name that would also appear on the residents register for this house and then I found it!"

"It's strange to think of old Mario being the great-great grandson of nanny Annie; she was so young!"

"She must've been once, but then she had a long life, she lived to the age of 92. She was well off too. The house Mario inherited eventually, was actually built by Annie's son, who like his father was a successful merchant in the fruit and veg business."

"And Mario is the last of the family?" asked Sylvia.

"No, there is a nephew, but he lives elsewhere with his wife and children. He is in the space navy. My late husband knew him, they were together on the Earth-Mars run," Sophia explained matter-of-factly, but obviously did not care to dwell more on the subject, changing it completely with her next sentence: "did Julian tell you about his plan to organise a séance in an attempt to contact the spirit world?"

They waited on Adrian's return before organising that séance. Julian had stated that he wouldn't do anything before Rip's return for, quote: "he wouldn't miss for the earth the expression on the fellow's face when facing that ghastly figure again"; the real reason being of course of rather more technical provenance: some of Julian's equipment had to be repaired or replaced as a result of the incredible power surcharge it was subjected to. Julian himself didn't mind – in the name of science, one is prepared to risk a lot more than that.

It was night again, but there was a full moon this time, shining reassuringly through the windows and besides Sophia and Sylvia had lit a goodly amount of candles in case the other lights went off.

"I don't think it will appear this time," Adrian said.

Stretching on the sofa, he appeared relaxed and untroubled. Dressed all in black from tip to toe, his tight fitting trousers and knee high leather boots completing his Shakespearian costume, he seemed completely at ease in the guise of the brooding Hamlet, he wanted to portray. Looking in Sylvia's admiring eyes, he felt ready for any challenge that might come his way.

Once again they were all sitting in the drawing room, with the door towards the entrance hall left wide open, for it was precisely in the entrance hall where the ghost had materialized the first time. Julian was still in his laboratory trying the same experiment as before.

"Shouldn't we sit in a circle and hold hands? Surely that's how they used to invoke the spirits in the past," suggested Sylvia.

"My dear girl, we live in the future now, we are supposed to keep up with the times," retorted Adrian with a laugh, "the apparitions of today or shall I say tomorrow, will be accustomed to the new methods too and won't be expecting the old fashioned medium. But here comes Julian. It seems to me it hasn't worked."

Then raising his voice he added in an exaggerated theatrical manner:

"Where are you, mysterious spectre?"

Adrian had timed it well. He hadn't even finished his sentence, when the now familiar apparition started slowly to materialise in front of them in all his phosphorescent splendour, still wearing the same Roman style toga and the same anachronistic watch. This time they were better prepared and did not find the experience so frightening. The spectre looked around and seemed pleased to find himself the focus of attention:

"Well, this time it worked properly."

His voice sounded to them not unlike the one on Rufus's emitter, and then they realised it *was* coming from the emitter, for the dog was not likely to make such statements.

"Hmm, hmm," he cleared his voice or more likely was testing the emitter, "please to meet you, folks! Is this a suitable greeting?"

"Hello will suffice," was Julian's riposte.

"Don't be so edgy, Julian! I am not very good at etiquette, I never was," the apparition pleaded, "oh, never mind, let's move to the next stage. I haven't frightened you this time have I?"

"Happily we were prepared for your... hmm... arrival," declared Adrian, "Julian here..."

The apparition waived a hand:

"I know all about Julian, he is my hero. I came here especially to meet him, and Sophie of course," he added as an afterthought, "how do you do, Sophie?"

"I am very well, thank you, but who are you?"

"Well, I am..." he looked a bit at a loss for words, then summoning his courage, blurted out all of a sudden, "your great-great-grandson, I am Trajan, come all the way from the future to meet you."

The silence that followed was caused chiefly by embarrassment, for nobody quite knew what to say, but Trajan interpreted it as a sign of doubt and hastened to explain:

"It's true! I can show you the DNA evidence here!"

He started to fiddle with his watch which also appeared to be some sort of communicator.

"You sent us a message," said Sophia, eventually.

Trajan brightened:

"Yes, I did! You can't imagine what this whole experience means to me! It did not quite work the first time round and I decided to watch out for another one of Julian's experiments to give me a chance to materialize. It's not as easy as you might think and I don't have much time either! I'll have to go soon. But before then..."

He suddenly flung himself towards Sophia in an attempt to embrace her, an attempt that failed miserably of course because Trajan had completely forgotten that he had arrived simply as a projection; an attempt which left everyone even more embarrassed than before.

"There, there," Sophia said soothingly as if addressing a child or a dog and waved her hands in an appeasing way, "it's all right, everything's all right."

"Let's not get too emotional, Trajan. It's all come as a bit of a shock," added Julian, "can't you send us more messages to explain the whole story to us if you haven't got the time to do it now?"

"Oh, I will, I will!" Trajan promised readily, "but there is so much to tell! Julian's Time Bubble Theory has been the cornerstone of my research and has made this Link possible and also a Link with the Future. This is an historic moment and that's why I find it so difficult to stay calm. Ever since I was a child, I was inspired by Julian and proud to be one of his descendants. I am so happy to be able to follow in his footsteps and to prove that I am worthy of him, of both of you. I'll go now! I love you all!"

He suddenly disappeared, leaving behind him utter confusion.

"Now, that tops it all!" Adrian said a couple of minutes later and as nobody replied, he got up and helped himself to a generous measure of Sophia's superior cognac, a goodly amount of which still remained in the old dusty bottle.

THE ULTIMATE LINK

The candles glimmered as if blown by the wind. Only there wasn't any wind. Sophia, Julian, Sylvia and Adrian were all seated in the drawing room expecting Trajan to appear as he'd done before. But instead of him another figure materialised in front of them, wearing even more unusual gear. The long hair was arranged to form a sort of halo around the head, and the face had unmistakably feminine features. The fair visitor walked around, stepping like a ballet dancer and stared at them unabashed.

"So! You are the Ancients!" she said at last, using Stuart's sound box, because Rufus, the dog, whose sound emitter Trajan had previously used for communication, wasn't in the room. He was sleeping no doubt in someone's bed, blissfully unaware of the excitement he was missing.

Not happy however with her new-found rich tenor voice, the new apparition gave Stuart a command which the robot instantly obeyed, changing his settings till he'd got a more appropriate contralto tone. The others were watching the proceedings with interest.

"Well, that's a bit better, everything considered. Now I can present myself. My name is Titania. According to the records, it appears that you are my ancestors. And by the Starry Heaven, what a bunch of weirdoes you are!"

She pointed a forefinger that ended in a saw-shaped golden nail towards Sophia.

"You! Turn to the right so I can better see your hairdo!"

But Sophia appeared somewhat inflexible and said she wouldn't oblige:

"You may issue commands to the robot, but not to me. Have you not been taught that you should show some respect to your elders?"

137

Titania was taken aback by this response and looked somewhat perplexed.

"Evidently not," continued Sophia blatantly, "decidedly you lack manners, my dear grand-daughter or whatever you are. What a shame. Such genes couldn't have come from me."

"Why should I show respect to my elders?" asked Titania at last, appearing genuinely surprised at the notion, "do you respect yours?" she added, looking at Sylvia.

"Of course!" replied Sylvia quickly, "what do you think?"

"But why? They are old fashioned on the whole and they haven't got a clue about the world of the young. They don't know anything about anything."

"But that's not true. They have also been young once and know only too well what it is like. My Gran for example, she always understood how I felt. She was my best friend and I miss her so."

"So what, she was your role model then?"

"I wouldn't say that. But she certainly set an example for me to follow. She was very talented and she convinced me that I had it in me too. But that's not all. Adults like Gran have also the experience which you and I are lacking."

"What experience?" Titania frowned. "It was all different when they were young. For a start they brought that plague that we are still struggling with."

"What plague?" asked Julian alarmed.

Titania turned towards him: "Granddad! Is that you?"

"I haven't got a clue," he replied. "Obviously you know better, young lady. I am just an old man who doesn't know anything about anything."

She suddenly smiled and this smile made her look more human:

"You are not that old and I like you, Granddad!" She added as an afterthought: "When I say Granddad, we are in fact several generations removed, if I want to be precise! But I like you! You don't look anything like the people in my time."

She went to him and tried to touch his face with her fingertips, forgetting that this was not possible. Julian couldn't feel her touch, but looked rather discomfited. Titania sighed, disappointed.

"Isn't that prickly?" she asked, pointing to his late afternoon stubble.

At this point Adrian started to laugh, seeing the expression on Julian's face:

"My dear Titania, are you telling me that you haven't ever seen your men unshaven?"

"Unshaven? What is unshaven? Is he unshaven?"

"I see, your males don't like body hair then," Adrian summed it up, "interesting."

"Men have the same skin as women," answered Titania, "smooth and silky."

"No body hair at all?"

"Of course not. Have you got any?" she gazed at Adrian eagerly, while he unbuttoned his shirt and proudly exposed a hairy chest.

"Wow! Starry Heaven! I have never ever seen anything like it." Again she stretched her hand to touch, but realising the futility of such an attempt, let it drop quickly but without letting her gaze fall. Sylvia wasn't very pleased and spoke abruptly:

"Never mind the hair, what about that plague?"

Titania reluctantly looked away:

"The plague," she shrugged her shoulders, "it was brought from space, wasn't it. That's always been a problem. Other lesser epidemics had already occurred as a result of negligence, but this one was extremely serious. It spread fast and soon reached disastrous proportions: 1/10 of Earth's population was wiped out as a result. The Space plague is still not entirely eradicated, but we are getting there. You were just talking about your grandmother. Well, I don't know mine, or my parents for that matter. Since the plague, AR (artificial reproduction) has been introduced across the world.   The embryos of course had to be developed in laboratory conditions, to make sure that all babies were immune and were absolutely healthy.   Cryogenic preservation of the surplus embryos was established to keep Earth's population to a set number. The whole way of life on Earth apparently changed from that moment, or at least that's what they say. For me, it's the only life I know."

"What about the other colonies?" asked Julian, "The Moon, Mars?"

"They won't have anything to do with us these days. We are still in quarantine, you see.   Space exploration has been suspended for the time being, I am sorry to say. At least from the Earth."

"So you don't have any contacts with the Lunar colony?" asked Sophia.

"To all intents and purposes no. We have enough on our hands as it is. What with the social unrest and the production issues…"

"But what about the helium that was mined on the Moon? Don't you need it anymore?" Julian asked surprised.

"Well, we've found other sources of energy. That is, we make more efficient use of solar, wind and water energy, convert all our waste into energy etc., but I am not an expert in this sphere, so I can't enlighten you more," replied Titania. "But it's my turn to question you now. Tell me are you happy to live in a family unit?"

Seeing that the others were exchanging glances, she added:

"I mean, what is it like?"

"You can't choose your family, but thank God you can choose your friends, that's what they say," Adrian replied eventually, grinning.

"Don't listen to him," cut in Julian, "he is a nob, he doesn't know better."

"What is a nob?" asked Titania puzzled.

"A nobleman, an aristocrat; and their families have been known to be more dysfunctional than any other. But never mind that," interjected Sophia, "a good family is the best environment to bring up children, if that is what you want to know. You need your parents and siblings for support and company, because we humans are social animals, we need an audience; we can't make it on our own. So if you are about to eradicate that plague of yours, think about resuscitating the old family values as they once were and you might find life changing for the better."

Sylvia listened, her amazement growing:

"But, Sophie, I thought you didn't get on with your parents! I thought…"she stopped tongue-tied under Sophia's eloquent glance, "oops! I wasn't supposed to say that, was I?"

Titania smiled again:

"It's all right! I know it anyway! I come from the future, don't I? I've seen Saskia and Ed before they went to the Moon. I am curious to go there actually, I've never been on the Moon, I mean in body, and I have to admit I envied them a bit. But Saskia and Ed are all right really," she looked at Sophia, "you miss them terribly, don't you? And you feel resentful because you think they've abandoned you. But they thought it was for the best. The trouble is that they do not rate themselves as the best of parents and they believed you were much happier to stay here, where you were born, with your grandparents, who you adored. Some people just don't know how to deal with children. They were guilt ridden of course, but this couldn't be helped. So that's why they buried themselves in their work. Don't judge them too harshly."

Titania then turned to Julian, leaving Sophia to reflect on this revelation.

"What about you?" asked Titania, "do you hold the same views?"

"Why, yes. I've been rather lucky to have been born in a nice middle class family and to have been given a pretty good education. Well, my father would've preferred me to follow in his footsteps, for he is quite a well-known architect, but I decided to pursue a different career path and he was happy enough with it."

"It's for the best you did what you did, otherwise…"

Titania didn't finish her sentence, but added instead:

"Trajan says that he took his inspiration from you, Julian; if it wasn't for you he wouldn't have gone into this particular field at all. There was no money in it, for a start, but he stuck at it regardless."

"What's your relationship with Trajan?" asked Sophia.

"He's my great great-grandfather," replied Titania, and I am pleased to have him and you of course in my family tree. I could've done a lot worse. But I've got to go now. I'd love to stay chatting longer, but I'll come back again soon! And, by the way, you have to tell me what milk is."

"What? You don't have milk in your century!" Sophia exclaimed rather startled, but Titania had already disappeared.

"There she goes! There goes our future," announced Adrian.

"Like always, stating the obvious!"

Sylvia was still a bit irritated by Titania's familiarity with her fiancé. He held her hand and kissed it affectionately:

"Don't tell me you are jealous, my love!"

"No, I am not!"

"Yes, you are!"

"Kids, it's getting late, let's finish this pantomime and go to bed, I've had enough excitement for one night," said Julian.

"I have to have a drink first!" protested Adrian.

Sophia started to blow out the candles and Sylvia got up and joined her, shaking her head:

"Men!"

"My, dear, lots of things might change with the passing of time, but human nature always remains the same."

"There!" exclaimed Julian, "the wisdom that comes with the years speaks now! There is no substitute for it, it comes with the white hair and you, you young people should take care! One day when you reach our age…"

Sophia tried unsuccessfully to conceal her laughter.

"Julian, keep this tirade for Titania's next visit," Sylvia interrupted him unceremoniously, "and work on the rhymes! You'll impress her even more!"

"And you were the one telling her to respect her elders, you ungrateful little brat, who won't even let me finish my sentence! Young people today…"

"Oh, Julian, don't lecture me now!" she replied giggling, "I'll be good, I promise. I'm going to bed now. Good night!"

With an exaggerated curtsey, Sylvia ran out of the room. Adrian followed her, forgetting all about his drink. Julian poured drinks for Sophia and himself and ushered her into the library, their favourite evening haunt.

The library had changed considerably since the times of Zara and Philip. Once it was full of bookshelves stacked with volumes in different languages: literature – fiction, documentaries, reference materials, maps – old and new. Most of them were now gone, scattered here and there or just destroyed by age. Real books made of paper had become rare and the remaining ones were usually kept in glass cases in which a specific temperature was maintained to preserve them from the elements. Sophia was the only one to open them occasionally and never without wearing gloves. The library still remained a library though and with the latest computer terminal recently installed, one had easy access to any book ever written. At least that's what the WLOL's (World Library OnLine) slogan said to reassure its readers.

Sophia had tried hard to recreate the cosy ambience this room had once retained, looking for inspiration at old photos and records, showing the room when it was first completed. She had largely succeeded, notwithstanding the difficulties and despite the fact that there was still a hint of the more clinical approach to interior design so prevalent in her time. The stylish, but comfortable armchairs upholstered in warm and homely colours, were arranged around an old fireplace, which had been preserved in its original state. The screens on the walls were loosely covered in fabric when not in use, something seldom seen in contemporary houses.

"At last some peace and quiet," Julian murmured suppressing a yawn as he settled into his armchair.

Sophia, irresolute, stood in front of him.

"What's the matter?" he reached for her arm, drawing her gently towards him till she was sitting on his knee, his fingers distractedly playing with her hair.

"Julian?"

"Yes, my dear."

"Are you sure, absolutely sure, that we are not changing the future in any way?"

He didn't reply immediately, but continued to stroke her hair.

"I am not. How can I? Only God Almighty knows. But I tell you this: if we are changing it, it's for the better."

"I wish I had your optimism."

"There is no reason why not. You've seen something of your future now, it might not be what you would have expected, but these things don't come with guarantees. In any case, this young lady knows how to look after herself."

"You mean Titania? But I wasn't referring to her, and yes, I am sure she will be alright. No, I was thinking about her world. What a place that might be, in the aftermath of widespread epidemics, where, I mean when milk (and presumably cows) have vanished from the face of the earth or where, or when the young don't care for their elders and everything is judged on appearances..."

"But humankind has been through such calamities before. You know that, you are a historian. Look at the big picture. We see just the fragments, bits of a puzzle that we are not able to see in its entirety. Whatever the situation I believe that our race will survive, it has proved its tenacity on countless occasions. Finish your drink, my dear and let's go

to bed. At least you know that one day we'll have a child, that is if we are to have grandchildren in the future."
Sophia put her empty glass on the table and smiled at him: "That might be sooner than you think."

Upstairs in her bedroom, furnished in the distinctive style of the 21 century, the century when Sylvia was born and lived most of her life, the young girl was getting ready for bed. She got herself comfortably under the warm covers, her dark-haired head was lying on the downy pillow. She was thinking about the future:
"I wonder if someone is watching me right now," she mused, "what if actually my future self is stealing a peep and recollecting all the excitement I have had recently. I hope I am not going to grow up to become fat and silly and boring like some. I would like to have a life that I would look back on with pleasure in my old age." More and more sleepy she stretched her hand and switched her bedside lamp off.

Outside, gazing at the starry sky, Adrian was also reflecting on the recent events. Rufus, an indistinct shape in the darkness, was making the last inspection of the grounds for the day.
"What will tomorrow bring?" wondered Adrian. "Funny! Before the Deep freeze, my life was absolutely boring. I was rich and spoilt. Even when I knew I was dying, it was still the same. I wish I had some revelation or something to wake me up. Today I look forward to each new day. I find each moment exiting and meaningful. What has happened to me? Has the Deep Freeze affected me in such way? Is it Sylvia? Or is it something in the air? Whatever it is, I hope it will stay, it will remain with me from now on. Come on, Rufus," he said aloud, "it's time to go to bed."
And with Rufus at his heels, he turned his back to the darkness and entered the welcoming and well lit entrance hall of "Elounda".

APPENDIX

Extracts from Zara's diary
("Elounda" Archive)

14th March 201x

At last started reading the historical novel I was so keen on. It's set in Tudor times. Quite a violent period, dramatic changes! Very interesting! The writer is a well known novelist, with a degree in historical literature. Bound to be good.

Little Sylvie is playing just outside with Philip. They get on together splendidly; bearing in mind that he'd never showed any particular interest in our son and daughter when they were young. Perhaps he's mellowed in his old age. Or perhaps there is something more to it. Jonathan is not unlike him and there is a certain reserve and stubbornness in his character too which makes communication between those two difficult.

Charlotte on the other hand has never been the charming little girl that would make her Daddy melt. To this day she lacks self-confidence and is shy and retiring. Perhaps I should've been less strict with her. But it's too late now. It can't be helped. She is coming soon for a couple of weeks with little Jamie. He will make a good playmate for Sylvie, I am sure. Thank God Adam is not coming; under the pretext that he is extremely busy. Still! I shouldn't grumble. At last I have the chance to spend a few days with my daughter and my grandson, something which doesn't happen that often because Adam always insists on going for their holidays to some "exotic", "tropical paradise" kind of places - the Caribbean, the Seychelles and the like. Cote d'Azur is not exotic enough for his taste.

17th March 201x

I am still reading the Tudorian novel. It's been rather disappointing though. Started with such anticipation only to discover that in depth knowledge of that historical period and the ability to write lightly are not enough to produce a really good read. All right! The writer is our contemporary; she can't help it if she narrates it from a modern point of view.

And yet there are things that a professional writer has to take into account. A novel written in the first person from the point of view of a young adolescent girl has to sound exactly like that, reasonably innocent; a girl should not express the cynicism and understanding that is to come later.

There is no development of her character either. From the beginning to the end she thinks and acts in the same way as if the experience of many years hasn't taught her a thing.

Girls and women in general were not treated as equals in those times, the way it's shown here; they owed obedience to fathers and husbands and those of them wise enough, kept their own council. Their feelings and desires were not taken into account; they were used to complying with the wishes of their elders from an early age.

Religion played a lot greater role than today, a lot greater than it's shown here.

Out of well known historical figures the writer has created melodramatic caricatures which might well appeal to romantic teenage girls, but don't convey any real feeling of the period in question or give you any real insights into the political situation of the time.

As for the language, it leaves a lot to be desired. Ladies talking like old hags at the fish market stalls? Somehow it doesn't ring true to me.

What makes a book a bestseller? It's difficult to tell. It all depends on the prevailing trends, the mood of the times. I am never going to write a bestseller anyway probably because I won't cater to the current fashion, I won't try to appeal to the wider masses and their fickle tastes. I write for my family and friends and to leave something behind, for posterity. I'd rather do it to my own set standards than pandering to the whims of others.

I have to go now. Little Sylvie has just come in and wants me to help her to pull open her Russian doll.

18th March 201x

I am sitting on the patio, enjoying the early morning sun and day-dreaming. Somebody behind me is pushing the French doors wide open:
"Mother!"
"Jonathan?"
"What *is* this?" he asks waiving a book under my nose.
"Why, it's my Tudor novel! I can't believe you are reading it! What do you make of it?"
"Of course I am not reading it! But someone else is! And I hate to say this to you, Mother, but I am not at all impressed with you. Such books as this one, that are at best questionable reading material for adults, should not be left lying around when there are impressionable young children about with minds easily corrupted by unsupervised reading," he waived the book in the air with disgust, "and I have to tell you that this is not something I am going to tolerate!"
I looked at him in utter amazement:
"What on Earth are you talking about?"

"I am talking about the books in this house!"

"But Jonathan, this is just a historical novel!"

"Historical or not, the vile language used here is not something I would appreciate my daughter getting acquainted with. Is it normal do you think for a little girl to ask what a miscarriage means? Or what the lady had in mind when she referred to "feeling his hardness"? For shame mother, I thought you knew better!"

"Really? This is a bit rich coming from you! If I am not mistaken you were already using at least half a dozen swear words that you'd learned from your mates when you were Sylvie's age!"

"It's different when you are a boy."

"Is it? In what age are you living, my boy? We've past the Victorian times. Young people of today are a lot more sophisticated than you give them credit for. Sylvie is rather smart and has an inquisitive mind. It's better to be told the truth about the birds and the bees at home rather than hear it from her peers all twisted and distorted."

"Don't lecture me, Mother! As it happens, I don't subscribe to your views. You had your chance with Charlotte and me. Now let me bring my children up the way I believe is right for them." And chucking the thick volume in my lap as if it was going to burn his fingers, Jonathan withdrew, with an angry flash in his eyes.

I had to write this little altercation in its entirety exactly as it happened. Its place is not here, in my diary, but I feel so frustrated and Philip is not around at the moment to confide in. The truth is that I don't get on with Jonathan. Whatever I do, it seems I can never reach him. Sometimes I wonder if this is the same little boy who would sit in my lap and listen with wide open eyes to the bedtime stories I used to tell him. How did he grow up to become so narrow-minded and pompous?

2nd April 201x

Charlotte and Jamie arrived and I am very pleased to see them. Charlotte looks a bit tired and depressed, but Jamie has grown up quite a bit since I last saw him and as I expected is having a lot of fun with Sylvie and Philip. They are playing badminton on the lawn right now.

I wish my daughter in law was here too, but she never is. These days young mothers are not that bothered if they have to go away and leave the children behind. Their priorities have shifted. We are lucky to have found Annie, Nanny Annie as Sylvie and Mat call her. She is great with the kids. But I am sure Celine will regret it one day. The kids are very fond of Annie; too much so I think…But I don't want to interfere. I don't think it's right. And Jonathan will resent it.

16th April 201x

Philip and I are just back from the airport. Charlotte and Jamie left for London and we already miss them. But they enjoyed their stay. And Charlotte looks a lot better now – more relaxed and content. Celine is still away, on a "yacht with friends", Jonathan said. I wonder…She hasn't rung once to enquire after the children. Jonathan doesn't confide in me. I suspect however that things are not going well there. I hope the children won't suffer if their parents split up.

17th April 201x

Funny the thoughts some seemingly unrelated article can provoke when one is so preoccupied with a particular subject. Philip was reading something about artificial reproduction (God knows what drew him to this topic) and came up with some remarks about ethical issues, biological parents etc. A lively discussion resulted out of that and although rather outraged by the mere idea of humans playing gods again, I had to admit that there were some positive aspects of it. Today we live in a world where adoption is made extremely complicated for infertile people, desperate to have children, while it seems, the ones that don't care are blessed to have them like it or not. To become a driver, you need a licence, to become a parent, you just need a partner.

I tried to imagine a society where people were created *in vitro* and then were born in and brought up in specific institutions by specifically trained and caring people, rather than by parents too busy with their lives; a society where the health and the interest of the child were a priority; where the term "orphanage" had an entirely new meaning and child trafficking or child abuse didn't exist any more...

And then there is another issue, the genetic engineering of embryos. Once it becomes possible, every parent will want a designer baby. But will the human race on the whole become smarter, healthier, better looking? Creating a super race; they have tried it in the past and it never worked. Is it going to work this time? It sounds too good to be true, but then again...who knows, perhaps in the future life might change in such a way. A whole new set of problems will arise then, naturally, but when there are problems, there are always solutions.

5th August 201x

Celine is off again. I am sorry to say that I confronted her before she went. Not that it made the slightest bit of difference. But I had promised myself not to interfere at all. However it can't be helped now. What is done can't be undone but I have the irresistible urge to write it down on paper because with the passing of time things often become strangely muddled. Having a record of what has passed between us, also is important from another point of view; if things go terribly wrong in this family, what am I saying, they are already bad enough, but if these two go their separate ways, is what I mean, I don't want to feel any guilt what so ever for contributing to the break-up. Anyway, so here goes:

I met Celine as she was calmly letting herself out with her Vuitton suitcase in her hand and couldn't help myself saying: "Off again, my dear? Are you not going to take the children for once?"
She looked at me disdainfully:
"What are you and Philip going to do by yourselves if I take them with me? Besides that doesn't concern you. It's between Jonathan and me."
"I see," I replied as coolly as I could, "if Jonathan is happy with this arrangement, Philip and I have to accept it too? A modern marriage? Or perhaps you might consider a separation?"
Celine put her suitcase on the floor:
"No, Zara! Don't expect too much. We are not going for a divorce. Not in the foreseeable future anyway. Is that clear? And I don't want any more discussions on this topic. It's none of your business."
She left me there speechless. I went to find Philip and told him. He raised his eyebrows after hearing my story and sighed:
"Well, you did what you could, let her be now. We're better off without her."
"But, Philip! These children need a mother!"
"They have you, my darling!"
"It's not the same. I'm their grandmother."
"There is Annie. Don't forget her."

"I know we can rely on Annie, but still. She is too young, she doesn't have any pedagogical experience, besides she is just a nanny."

"Not exactly Mary Poppins then?" said Philip with a twinkle in his eye.

"Hardly. Sylvie is about to start school and is struggling with her French; what a shame - it's her mother tongue and yet although she speaks it fluently, she can barely read and makes a lot of spelling mistakes. Matt will have the same problems when he starts school."

"It's too bad. I can't help her. My French is no better than yours. I am afraid I still make lots of mistakes. Find a private teacher if you think that will help matters. Do whatever you think is necessary, you have my full support."

"Yes, you are right, Philip. I'll think about it."

20th September 201x

We've settled into a routine now. The children go to school. When they are back, we all get involved in homework, lessons and games...When I say "we", I mean Philip, Annie and me. Jonathan is at work and as for Celine...she is hardly ever at home. She appears and disappears for her "modelling sessions", parties, auditions etc., kissing absentmindedly the children when she encounters them somewhere, patting Jonathan affectionately on the cheek, as if he is a dog, and glaring at Philip and me if we accidentally bump into her. But she is less and less at home, so we don't have to suffer her presence very often.

10th October 202x

We are going to Crete for our wedding anniversary. Haven't been there since our honeymoon. Yet we've often promised ourselves to go there again and explore the island. So many memories from that trip, the happiest in our lives perhaps. We were young and the world was our oyster. Well, we have made it. But it wasn't easy; there were plenty of disappointments and frustrations on the way. There were tears. But it's always the case, isn't it? Everything you get comes with a price.

Now the children are grown up and even the grandchildren don't need us so much these days, so we can afford to spend more time together, just the two of us. Our life is entering calmer waters at long last after the hectic times we'd been through.

What are we going to make of the island after all these years? Is it much changed, I wonder? At the time we thought it was somehow in a time warp, still in the 50s, modern technology coyly and tentatively getting its hold there. Unspoilt by mass tourism, or almost.

In those times I needed a visa to get there of course. Not any more. Now I am a citizen of Europe. Not that much has changed, of course. I feel no more European than I ever did - being born in a geographical region of Europe, that's hardly surprising. At least now, as part of the big European family, the frontiers are open and, I suppose, in a way there is more freedom. Well, just about. To be fair, there is less bureaucratic hassle when travelling across Europe. Less border check points.

Borders! Who needs them? What's the point of them? For a tiny minority, called the governing body, to be able to restrict people and make them obey the immigration laws created by them. Divide and rule! A strategy that has worked millennia. Why change it?

Political borders are there to keep people who want to get out in and those who want to come in – out. Who do these restrictions benefit? Local people? Hardly. Would the immigrants stop coming if they were to tighten the border control? Unlikely. Wouldn't they take the jobs from the locals? Well – only if there are jobs for the taking. Not to put too fine a point on it but, there are also the language limitations; the newcomers are at a disadvantage there for a start. How was it before all this bureaucratic palaver came to be, anyway? Before the border controls were introduced?

But anyway, I got rather carried away. As I said at the time of our honeymoon, which was in fact last century, last millennium even, I needed a visa to go to Crete. Now I just need an identity card. I wonder how I will feel this time.

After all these years it's still so vivid in my mind. I remember so well our time there as if it was yesterday: the late night arrival, the torrential rain, otherwise so rare on Crete, the challenging drive along the slippery winding road…And then the next day the skies were clear, the air was fresh and the sun was shining above the beautiful Bay of Marbello, the breathtaking view of which we observed first thing in the morning from our windows.

The ambience of Elounda was exactly what we needed at the time; the fishing port, the taverns and coffee shops and the sandy beach where we would cool our excitement in the blue waters of the Aegean.

Now we live on another Mediterranean coast, on the Cote d'Azur. We built the house we always wanted here, but called it "Elounda" in an attempt to retain something of that happiness which we experienced there on Crete. It is a joyful house, but life here is just not the same. Nothing ever is.

The town of Elounda won't be either when revisited and I have serious misgivings about going there again. But Philip wants to go and he desperately needs a holiday. He hopes we'll be able to recapture those happy, lazy, carefree days we had there. Let's hope for the best. Let's hope we won't be disappointed. In a way it's going to be like a trip back in time.

30th November 202x.

My heart is mute and I can't even grieve properly. My Sylvie is gone and I shall never see her smiling face again. They tell me that the Deep Freeze is not Death. They say there is hope. I don't see the difference. What is death for you if not the loss of a loved one? The soul is immortal but the person you knew is gone.

The house is so unusually quiet. Even Matt is behaving, something unusual for him. I can't talk to Philip. He wanders aimlessly about the grounds, trying to come to terms with recent events. At long last I can talk to Jonathan. Our loss has brought us together for the first time in years. Celine is not much help. She has bottled the pain inside and will be off again soon, in the vain hope that she can run away from it.

Bereaved, we all suffer, each in our own way.

Extract from the "New Age Vedapedia" (post Space-Plague edition of the Wikipedia)

Titania and her times

In the aftermath of the space plague, humanity had to ensure its survival. The AR (artificial reproduction) was introduced as the only method of reproduction and society had to change accordingly. The family unit disintegrated entirely. Children were brought up together in crèches and never knew their parents or their siblings. Later on, when adults, they were allowed access to the records and were able to trace their families, but this was not encouraged and more often than not ended in disappointment. The lack of family meant that each individual had to fend for themselves and in order to succeed, friendships and alliances were formed.

This new way of life caused new problems to emerge and with them new conflicts and power struggles. Power shifted constantly from one influential political group to another, each trying to make its own mark, trying to establish a long lasting legacy. That rarely happened. The lessons from history forgotten, the same old mistakes were being made again and again, and totalitarian regimes were replacing democratic ones which in turn gave way to more liberal ones.

People as always found totalitarian regimes too oppressive, a society with their civil liberties curbed, but the democratic ones opened the door to anarchy, becoming too chaotic and the government unable to cope with the escalating violence and crime.

Like the others, Titania was born in a laboratory and brought up in the same way as her contemporaries. When she finally had access to the records, she found out that hers was an illustrious family, for she belonged to the line of Julian Bradley. This must have boosted her confidence, for she suddenly emerged as a leader from amongst her comrades.

Titania was a member of a group of young people who grew up together and who were interested in evolution and history. They called themselves the connectionists and their particular group was called Connect for Knowledge and Success, shortened to CKS. They participated in the Link regularly, going back to different time coordinates and gradually started to see some patterns emerging. The connectionists wanted these patterns analysed and used to create contemporary models which could then be used to form a new world order.

They were very enthusiastic as young people usually are, and believed they had the answer. But theirs appeared as a very controversial agenda and they had opponents, calling themselves the get-realists (from their motto "get real"), who maintained that history was irrelevant and proclaimed that looking into the past was a form of escapism, without any practical use whatsoever and at best a waste of time. Some extremists belonging to this second group, the radical get-realists were even prepared to attack the Chrono-Bridge Centres and demolish them.

Titania was the one who established a two-way Link with her great-great-grandfather Trajan, encouraging him to go ahead with his experiment and take the Link to a new level. She rightly assumed that an interaction with her ancestors would give her an insight into a way of life long forgotten, certain aspects of which she wanted to resuscitate and were an inspiration in her plans for decisive action. This historic contact, she argued, was to create a precedent and the foundation of inter-temporal relations.

Titania was not particularly concerned about creating paradoxes in the space time continuum. She believed that such paradoxes would automatically cancel themselves out when change occurred in line with the self-consistency principle. According to it, going back in time would not create paradoxes, the only possible time lines being those that are self-consistent; i.e. anything a time traveller might do must have been part of history in the first place.

Titania's provocative attitude towards her ancestors Julian and Sophia Bradley when she met them, was partly deliberate. She only had limited time with them, not at all sufficient for long discussions, thus her ingenious idea to stage it so as to get maximum information out of each session. What she wanted to see was a family unit in action, for her idea was to reintroduce it again, as the building block for their society, which she believed was falling apart by severing the ties between different generations.

It all worked out on more than one level. Bradley/Trajan's discovery, hitherto kept in secret, quickly became well-known across their respective worlds due to Titania's efforts. "Once the cat is out of the bag," she famously said, "there is no going back."

She was right. The way to defeat the get-realists was not to be by means of violence. The newly established Ultimate Link as it was called, was to become the latest trend, adopted by the elite, amongst whom Titania had already succeeded in finding numerous allies.

Bradley, Trajan and Titania certainly achieved fame, but whether they succeeded in their pursuit of happiness is not so clear. Fame is a blessing and a curse and an encounter with this lady hardly left one unscathed. Julian Bradley probably was the luckiest of them all because he had Sophia to keep him straight. Trajan got married again and produced the offspring who was to become Titania's great grandfather.

Titania became a world leader, the role she always coveted, but soon became disillusioned and retired from office. The "family unit ideal" she was striving for was not attained in her life time. But she succeeded in changing the ideas and attitudes concerning the biological origins of the individual, proving that they are significant to people.

The ancient philosophers spoke about the importance of self knowledge, she explained, but this self knowledge wouldn't be complete unless one knows the characteristics inherited from one's forefathers. The disappearance of the traditional family in post-Plague times, she stated, has undermined lineage and thus identity. And as social identity is based on biological ties, this identity naturally gets muddled and confused as a result, was her final conclusion.

She spent the rest of her life writing a philosophical treatise on the spiral properties of evolution and founded a philosophical school which had a large following.

www.ingramcontent.com/pod-product-compliance
Lightning Source LLC
Chambersburg PA
CBHW030551030726
47495CB00004B/1210